Blue Road to Atlantis

Blue Road to
ATLANTIS

JAY NUSSBAUM

WARNER BOOKS

An AOL Time Warner Company

Copyright © 2002 by Jay Nussbaum

Warner Books, Inc., 1271 Avenue of the Americas, New York, NY 10020

Visit our Web site at www.twbookmark.com.

 An AOL Time Warner Company

Printed in the United States of America

First Printing: July 2002
10 9 8 7 6 5 4 3 2 1

Library of Congress Cataloging-in-Publication Data

Nussbaum, Jay.
    Blue road to Atlantis / Jay Nussbaum.
        p. cm.
    ISBN 0-446-52821-8
    1. Blue marlin fishing—Fiction. 2. Atlantis—Fiction 3. Old age—Fiction 4. Fishes—Fiction. I Title.

PS3614.U87 B58 2002
813'.6—dc21   2001046646

To my wife, Betty.
To call you the woman of my dreams
would be to give undue credit to my imagination.
You are the miracle of my life and I adore you.

To my children, my bloodsoul,
Taylor and Brian.

And to my parents, Alice and Herbert,
who loved me enough to let me
find my own current.

ACKNOWLEDGMENTS

A man whose lifelong dream is to publish a book about lifelong dreams owes a unique debt of gratitude to those who helped to make the dream a reality.

First, my family, for molding what you could and accepting what was already molded long before we met: Bella (just around the corner), David, Richard, Sandy, Jennifer, Jessica, Joshua, Jake, Danielle, Carlos, Geraldine, Yesenia, Sandra, Sonia, Rey, Melissa, Kristen and Jess. Families are mutual universes. Sometimes you revolve around me and sometimes I revolve around you, and then sometimes we all just spin around bumping into stuff. I love you all.

I would next like to thank my editor, John Aherne. Adlai Stevenson once wrote, "An editor is someone who separates the wheat from the chaff and then prints the chaff." Maybe so, sometimes. But what separates the men from the boys is the guts to stride confidently into a Tuesday morning editorial meeting and pitch a book about talking fish. I cherish both your guidance and your friendship.

Of course, until my agent, Helen Breitwieser, took an interest in me, it was all just five manuscripts in a drawer. Thank you for your faith in me. The desperation and naivete of young authors make us easy prey for the many predators of the literary world. Your integrity, patience, extraordinary skill and, of course, friendship, mean the world to me.

Steve Maizes, I thank you for introducing me to Helen. Kurt Mahoney, I thank you for introducing me to Steve. Can't remember how I met Kurt.

Thank you to Dr. Tim Radomisli, my first gentle reader, and to Milda DeVoe, my second, considerably less gentle reader. You are more than a book doctor, Milda, but I don't think they call them wizards anymore, outside of Hogwarts. To David Finkelstein and Evelyn Letfuss, for your guidance, encouragement and friendship. *Sensei*, I'll never be the writer you are or the martial artist that you are. My hope is one day to be the man that you are. To Al Gantert, maybe not the smartest man at Cornell, but sure as hell the wisest. To Charlie Trezvant and Dr. John Sarno, who taught me how to care for my aching back, enabling me to sit and write for longer hours. To my friend and fellow author, Steve Samuel, author of *Rock, Paper, Scissors*. Remind me, Sammy, what exactly were we doing in law school?

And to the many others who have offered a hand, a kind word, or the like, I offer my most sincere thanks: Frances Jalet-Miller, Hillary Cohen, Dr. Fred Levy,

Manabu Kimura, Itzik Harel, Susan Aguado, Brandon Saltz, Tammy Ader, the entire Canaan family, David and Shari Herman, Katie Blough, Matthew Menchel, *Sensei* George Mattson, *Sensei* Robert Campbell, Carol Myer, David Lonner, Doug Greene, Pierce Hoover of *Sport Diving Magazine*, Albia Dugger and Chris Ronzoni. And finally, thank you to my old student, Drew Arenowitz, who abruptly became my teacher one day, when he stopped me in my tracks with the casual comment, "Every man chooses his freedom."

Freedom and slavery are mental states.
MOHANDAS K. GANDHI (1948)

Society often forgives the criminal;
it never forgives the dreamer.
OSCAR WILDE (1891)

Perhaps life is just that . . . a dream and a fear.
JOSEPH CONRAD (1911)

True enlightenment is within the fish.
JONAH

CHAPTER ONE

WATER IS LIFE. When it is warm, I am warm. When it is cool, I am cool. When it is clear, I am blessed with the vision of a seagull. When it is cloudy, I am blind. It passes over me as a salty abluent and cleans me in its shimmering beauty. It soils me too. It brings me the air that I breathe and the food that I eat. One day, I will be the food that it brings to feed another. The sound of water is silence; the sound of silence is the hum of posterity. The movement of water is stillness; the stillness is the current, the drift and the everlasting roll. Sound within silence and movement within stillness. And always, always, respect for the current. The ocean's current as well as the current that stirs within each of us.

I fly through the infinite, blue water as birds fly through the infinite, blue sky. After all, water is sky.

Compressed sky. One cannot exert pressure on water; pressure goes right through it and is dispersed. To pressurize water, it must be contained. But contained water is no longer water at all. Just as a spirit held under the thumb of another—or under the thumb of its own fears—is not truly a spirit, merely a stifled cry. Just so, the authentic water in this world of ours is the oceanic water and none other.

In the water, I have never felt any separation. It is my mother, father and life source. I am its child, its precious child.

Call me Fishmael.

I am now old and gray, but even when I was young and gray, I always dreamed of imparting to others my world of the sea. It is my heart I offer.

I am called a remora. Some call me a marlinsucker, but I have always detested that word. It implies things about my relationship with the Old Fish that are not the case.

I remember the day that my father informed me that I would be spending most of my life attached by my head to a marlin. At the time, I must admit, I considered the plan lacking in initiative. But my father showed me the oval-shaped groove at the top of my head and explained the concept of the suction cup. And he told me that he had lived on a marlin, as had his father before him, and I take no pause in proclaiming it a good relationship. A mutual relationship. I am no parasite, let that be clear. I clean the Old Fish's gills and skin, and in return, his skin-filth is my food. It is not my only food; marlin are notably sloppy hunters and feeders. The leftovers from his magnificent hunts are delicacies that, alone, I could never enjoy—octopod, small squid, filefish, crab, balao, mackerel, tuna— a pretty rough lot. Some might call it an uneven trade, but the Old Fish, he understands. He is my teacher.

Each to his own place, says the Old Fish. For he who knows his current and swims within it, prosperity is inevitable. Do not fret about who swims above you and who swims below. All swim above some and below others, except the flying fish, and they usually wind up on the bottom of some skiff with a stupid, surprised look on their face. Even the mighty sperm whale loses when he ventures too deep and suffocates in the tentacles of the giant squid.

Of course, the Old Fish did not always follow his own advice. It has been many years, and much water has since passed beneath our fins, but I still remember the day the Old Fish lost his beloved Migdalia to a fisherman's hook. A fisherman who proclaimed himself *El Campeón*, who dragged our poor Migdalia brutally from the water, though he knew full well that she would die in the air. After that, the Old Fish sounded into the depths of the ocean for years. Of course, I went with him. But that was long ago and today, we again swim in warm, lighted waters.

He is an old fish, massive and splendid to behold, with a broad purple back that fades to royal blue atop his head, and twelve lavender stripes that adorn his silver sides. His spear alone is bigger than most fish. His carriage is regal. He swims with majestic grace. He is the jewel of the seven seas.

His age does him honor. Age is a great accomplishment in the sea, where predators appear out of a blue cloud in the blink of a nictitating membrane. There is no drama to death in the sea; one moment one is there and then one is not. Families do not mourn; they scram. But the Old Fish has not cheated death. No, he has given it more than fair opportunity to take him. But he has always been stronger, faster, smarter.

And now in his old age, so revered is he that not a single fish would dare to challenge him. Even the sharks—mako, hammerhead, white—all respect him. The vulgar tiger shark, who feeds on everything including other tiger sharks, defers as we swim past. Only in the depths do enemies still exist for us . . . and of course, on the surface. Fisherman. The bane of Neptune's Kingdom. Why must they come out here? Why is almost every robust healthy boy with a robust healthy soul in him, at some time or other crazy to go to sea? Only an alien could so romanticize a land. Can they not see how ill-suited they are to the sea? When God wanted to finish them all off some time ago, what did He use? Drought? No, flood. If they need to hunt, why can't they hunt their own, as we do?

Today we are returning from our trip to the African coast. We had followed the frosty Benguela Current for days, my scales raw and frozen to my sides. Hearing my denticles chatter, the Old Fish had suggested that I suck onto his belly, but I declined, knowing that work would keep me warm. Yesterday, we finally emerged from the cold and were able to pick up the warmer Brazil Current. From here, we will follow the Pangean Fracture Zone, veer south around Cuba, catch the Caribbean Current and follow the Caribbean Basin to the Florida Current—our beloved Gulf Stream. Ah, the Gulf Stream, a raging river in the middle of the ocean. One barely needs even to use a fin in the Stream, as long as he follows the current. I am anxious to return to those warm, clear, sky blue waters.

But for now the water, though shallow, is still murky green. We pass a cleaner station, where blennies dart in and out of the gills of a nurse shark, who lies passively on the seabed as they work. She opens her mouth and four blennies swim in to clean the inside. It always amazes me that they can get away with that, swimming into the mouth of a shark, but such is their current. A school of coneys overtakes us excitedly, which fills me with anticipation. Sure enough, in time we see the huge mossy rock where the coneys gather by the thousands. We call it Coney Island, and I pull up alongside the shimmering, vertical stripes of the Old Fish to ask if we will be stopping to feed.

"Please," I urge him. "When will our next chance come to enjoy the footlongs?" But he is not paying attention.

"*Te lo juro por mi madre*, Fishmael," he is saying. "This is the year I do it. This is the year I make pilgrimage to Atlantis."

I have heard this vow for years.

"Yes," I reply dutifully, "this is the year."

"My current has led me many places, and always I have followed it faithfully. I have heard the call of Atlantis since we were young, Fishmael. Why something has always appeared to complicate matters and keep me from going, I cannot know. But this is the year."

"This is the year." I am still looking back over my dorsal fin toward the coneys.

"This is the year we swim past the complications, confusion and Sargasso weed; across the river and into the trees of the Narrows of Bimini, and seek out the Great Spotted Dolphins of Atlantis. And on the blue water of Atlantis, the Great Spotted Dolphins will teach me the sky, the air that until now I know only in the fleeting dreams of a jump. And when I attain Atlantis and know the sky, I will share my wisdom for the benefit of my brothers of the sea."

The gaze of his enormous, round eye has drifted far into the distance. Though I no longer believe that we will be going to Atlantis in this or any other year, I admire the Old Fish. His dream never dies, and this is the true source of his beauty. Outshining his two Aegean blue dorsal fins, tougher than his thick, granular flesh, more complex than the hexagonal scales imbedded in his silver flanks and darker than the deep purple of his back, his dream of Atlantis has been the Coriolis force of his life.

For days we swim in silence, following the current over reefs, cones and plateaus, toward the Gulf

Stream. Around us, the ocean is alive. A glorious opah nods as she passes us. Her seductive, red lips puckered in a perpetual flirt, she offers the traditional greeting: "Swim with the current, boys."

"Swim with the current," we reply.

Beneath us, tiny wrasses and blennies skip through the coral in search of food. We swim away from the reef. We too are hungry, and the Old Fish will not find any food of substance near the reef. I point out a variety of catfish sifting through the sand below. Gafftopsail catfish, hardhead catfish. The Old Fish is not interested. Fat snook, seahorses, slippery dicks.

"I see a school of timucu," I say.

"Too small."

This is always a source of tension between us. I can make a meal of anything, but the Old Fish is huge. The bigger the fish, the more it takes to fill it. The Atlantic blue whale ingests a million calories a day. And it shows.

It is getting dark. Neon green moray eels cautiously emerge from their lairs to begin their hunts. I see an octopus far below us, sliding along the reef, through narrow fissures, looking for prey. I know what we are waiting for.

"Tuna?" I ask.

The Old Fish smiles. "Yellowfin. I have been craving it all day."

We dive a bit deeper. Tuna seek cool waters when they sense a predator nearby. Somehow, they are able to stay warm even in cold water, which helps them to outswim us.

"Isn't it getting too dark to hunt this deep, Old Fish?"

"You may wait for me above," he says gently.

"I think I just saw a viperfish."

"Relax, Fishmael. There are tuna nearby; I sense it. We will catch a big one then return to the surface. There are no vipers here."

I hate it down here. Though we are not nearly as deep as I am imagining, our years in the depths have left me permanently scarred. In the depths, where food is a rare and unpredictable occurrence, the predators are of a fierceness that the fish of the suburban thermocline cannot even imagine. I see viperfish everywhere. I see their hideous, gaping maw and silver, crushed-glass eyes. They are the perfect predator, designed specifically to create death in the world around them. Curved, wretched fangs, so long and sharp that they are biologically incapable of closing their mouth. Jaws that open so wide they can devour a fish equal in size to themself. A heart that actually retracts during feeding, so as not to get in the way. And an insidious organ deep inside their throat that emits a soft, blue-green light, to lure prey. It is not their fault. Too many years evolving in deprivation, it could happen to anyone. But while I never see anything but the viper, the Old Fish never sees anything but the tuna.

"Come on," I plead, "let's get out of here."

But as I am speaking, the Old Fish accelerates upward with an astonishing burst of speed. He explodes into a school of tuna twenty fathoms above us, swiping his spear wildly back and forth. As always, I seek shelter in his gills and hold on as he stuns and smashes a half-dozen yellowfins. The survivors scatter to save themselves, abandoning their dead and injured. As I have said, we are not among God's more gallant creatures.

The Old Fish circles around and I stagger from his gills in time to see him take a dead tuna broadside, with such force that it folds in half as it disappears into his mouth. He takes a second one head first, and spits a piece of flesh for me.

For the rest of our swim along the thermocline toward the Gulf, the Old Fish is quiet. As we reach the western shore of Cuba, he slows and turns to me.

"I thought I heard cheering in my chest, Fishmael, as I was hunting the tuna. Were you cheering for me?"

"Of course."

"Please do not. It is unseemly to cheer the demise of others. If we lose, another survives."

"What if you are fighting an evil fish?"

"Then you may cheer, if you are sure it is I who is good and the other who is evil."

"You are always good."

"I am no better than my appetite; others are no worse than theirs. The cookiecutter shark I killed in Africa simply wanted to attach to my flank and bore out plugs of flesh to eat. Good and evil are phantoms, Fishmael; there is only desire, obstacle and appetite."

"Some appetites seem insatiable."

"True enough."

"What if you were fighting the Red Tide?" I ask, thinking of the rumors of a Red Tide advancing from the South Pacific.

The Old Fish laughs softly. "Red Tide kills millions. Should it ever be within my power to fight it, then you may cheer."

The sun is rising as we reach the western shore of Cuba and flow into the Florida Current. There is no wind. The sea-ceiling is still, and through it I see a blue sky. We rise to two fathoms, to feel the rays of sun that pierce the water and fan out over us. Honeycombs of sunlight dance across the coral and the Old Fish glances at me with mischief in his eye. I suck onto his pelvic fin, knowing he is about to leap.

But just as he curls his mighty tail, a fisherman's hook plops into the water. We have not been fooled by a baited hook since the one that stole our dear Migdalia, so we simply watch it as it descends past us. Amateurishly baited, the skewered sardine washes off the hook and they part company, the hook sinking, the fish rising. As the sardine floats toward us, the exposed silver point of the hook nicks a marlin egg that had been floating freely. A tiny droplet of oil seeps out of the egg, draining its buoyancy, and the egg too begins to sink.

I am horrified by the sight of the defenseless egg sinking toward the aphotic zone, and as I eat the sardine, a panicked female marlin appears and sounds after the egg. A young marlin—her son, I assume—follows close behind. The Old Fish inverts himself, aiming his head straight down, and I latch onto his tail.

He follows their downward path, all of us now trying to overtake the egg before it wanders into the depths. My gills are flooded by the onrushing water, and in seconds we are enshrouded in darkness.

As our eyes adjust to the grim surroundings, I see a faint blue-green light rushing toward us.

The mother and son confront the excited viperfish before we arrive. Only the mother floats between the viper and the egg. The viper's eyes are wide and crazed, aroused by the scent of the egg. In the light of those eyes, I see it kill her quickly. Eggs are the rarest of delicacies in the depths; the viper cannot afford to be denied. The boy flashes toward the egg, but is thumped away by the Old Fish, who squares himself to the viper. As always in moments of stress, his gills flare. As always, I scurry inside.

Peering out, I see a crowd begin to gather in the outer shadows. It is a terrifying circle. Spinythroat scorpionfish, dragonfish, giant squid. As a child, I had nightmares about coming home to surprise parties like this. A stonefish—the deadliest fish in the world—notices me in the Old Fish's gills and winks.

I motion to the boy to protect the egg and he gathers it to him and stays near the Old Fish.

Though I am concerned, I have seen the Old Fish do battle in the depths before. After Migdalia died and we sounded, war was like food to the Old Fish, and every day he sated his hunger.

I will never forget the day Migdalia died, when *El Campeón* tore a hook into her lovely mouth. Even now, I cannot think of the day without a pang of death in my heart. She was so gentle, her soul so still. Whenever the turbulent sea left me muddled and scared, I would go to her. Just being with her would calm me. "Hush, Fishmael," she would whisper, "it's only water."

As *El Campeón* trawled her mercilessly through the sea, the Old Fish stayed with the skiff the entire time, hiding his anguish from Migdalia, bodying up to her reassuringly. And when *El Campeón* finally ended her torture—plunging a gaff into her heart and pulling her into his skiff—still the Old Fish swam alongside. He could not abandon his Migdalia, but neither could he bring himself to jump, afraid of what he might see. Finally he jumped, me clinging to his belly, and we saw. Migdalia lay on the floor of the skiff, her eye dead and gone, her dazzling colors drained gray. The Old Fish did not say a word, but his mournful whimper broke me. His heart died that day no less than hers, and we sank for years into the depths.

There, he devoted himself to becoming the fighting equal of any deep-sea predator. He was and remains the greatest swordsman in the sea. So as I peer out now at our enemies, I am not afraid. We have survived the six-thousand-fathom Challenger Deep in the South Pacific and we lived through the Great Depression in the Indian Ocean. We will not die here.

This is why we learned the depths, so that we never again need fear the chaos of the sea; so that we could defeat any foe. We could have simply traversed the globe after Migdalia's death, but the Old Fish said there was nothing more to learn by swimming wide, that we must go deep. There is more water beneath every square foot of surface than one can imagine, and we have already found our light in the aphotic zone. No, we will not die here. As the Old Fish says, there are only two secrets in battle. One: Never be the last to know that a fight has begun. And two: Assume defeat but commit to victory. I have never quite known what that means, but he always wins, so I accept it.

The viper glares at us through its silver eyes, aghast that any fish would interfere with its hunt. With a hiss, it aims its gruesome fangs at the Old Fish and charges. The two smaller fangs that extend horizontally from its upper jaw pierce the skin of the Old Fish and tear out a line of flesh. Clearly, its heart has moved out of the way.

The Old Fish swipes with his spear and pounds the right flank of the viper, but it has little effect. The long, curved fangs of the viper lash back at the Old Fish and pass within inches of my cove. Suddenly, the Old Fish pauses. I have seen this pause before, whenever the savvy old warrior finds weakness within his enemy's greatest strength.

I cannot imagine what he has just realized, but now the Old Fish baits the viper, showing his meaty broadside. I am staring directly at the viper as it charges, its jaws wide. Just as it closes in, however, the Old Fish spins his giant body into an inversion, placing himself above the viper. With all of his might, he thwaps his spear down upon the viper's head, driving its jaws together. Each set of fangs impales the jaw opposite, and the viper's mouth is closed forever.

I enjoy the expressions of astonishment around us, as the viper swims away, harmless as a seahorse. The Old Fish always tells me that justice is too rare a dessert to be expected in a sea of saltwater. He says to expect dessert is to ruin the meal. But the taste of justice lingers sweet in my mouth today, and I savor it as I watch the viper disappear into the darkness. Evil is a current too, I think, albeit a vertical one.

B ACK IN THE LIGHT, the Old Fish sleeps as we pass the Gulf of Mexico. The orphaned marlin swims absently along with us. Though the current is with us, the swimming is slow, with the Old Fish asleep and the young marlin laboring with the egg tucked under his left pectoral fin. The child's eyes are elsewhere. There is no drama to death in the sea, but the aftermath—the abandonment—is the shock of a stingray's barb, as the poison of loss seeps slowly in. Loss is the sadness, not death. Death is an unplumbed mystery. Erosion, transformation . . . who can say? We know less of it than we know of the other side of the sea-ceiling. But of loss, we are well informed. We pass the survivors every day. Most of us are survivors ourselves. Loss is the piecemeal death of those still alive.

Some endure; some do not. Angelfish do not. They mate for life, then die within a day of each other.

The young marlin will live, though he is not exactly sure what that means anymore. Outwardly, he is neither angry or upset. But the waters of a shifting current are turbulent. The adjustment is a struggle. And now he must choose: Does he accept his change of circumstance, or does he swim against the inevitable tow until his fins tire and he is swept into a new direction nonetheless? It is often easier to realize one's current than to submit to it. Periodically, he glances at the egg. It is his responsibility now.

I ask him his name.

"Jotaro," he answers.

"You will swim with us now, Jotaro."

"I will swim alone."

"And do what for food? Your spear is not yet grown. You cannot hunt."

"I do not care."

"Then consider the egg. When it hatches, it will need food."

Jotaro does not answer. He is willful. He has decided to grow up, and seems to be experimenting with the current of the tortured loner. This would sadden me. We have all been bitten, abandoned and tagged; it does not excuse us our civic love. Worse, the current of the tortured loner reeks of conscious choice. A current is not something to choose; it is something to embrace when it chooses you.

By the time we reach the Gulf Stream, the sea is

an eddy of gossip. Sound travels fast in water, especially when that sound is a rumor. Word of the Old Fish's heroism precedes us, and as we glide into the Florida Straits, we are cheered. The Old Fish smiles magnanimously to the thousands of fish surrounding us, and I bob my head in acknowledgment. Though my part in the rescue was less flamboyant, my role in battle, as I understand it, is to stay out of the way. I take this responsibility seriously.

"Float like a jellyfish, sting like a jellyfish!" someone shouts.

"Three cheers for the Old Fish!"

Next to me, Jotaro is scowling.

The Old Fish beams, though he tries halfheartedly to deflect the praise. "Brothers," he says, "please. I did nothing that any of you would not do."

"Other than triumph," a jawfish mumbles through the eggs brooding in his mouth.

"How did you do it?" asks a glassy sweeper.

"The viper is not invincible." The Old Fish shrugs, but stops speaking suddenly and looks into the distance. A massive, black cloud is rushing toward us. It is a school of hammerhead sharks, hundreds of them, swimming in a tight, dark formation. I feel my body stiffen as I watch them approach like an oncoming storm.

The hammerhead looks vaguely like a bull shark that has swallowed a ship's anchor. With their eyes protruding from the sides of their T-shaped heads, they have no forward sight, and the school nearly crashes headlong into the crowd.

"It's coming!" one of them cries. "We have spotted the Red Tide off the south coast of Africa! It is sure to be here within two weeks!"

Panic sweeps through the crowd. Red Tide is a rare phenomenon, said to originate with the ripening of a mysterious coastal plant. It drifts relentlessly forward for hundreds of miles before dispersing, carrying a deadly bacteria that suffocates every fish in its broad path. The last Red Tide killed twenty million, approaching as a lovely pink bloom and leaving a wake of silence behind. We have always been helpless against it. But then again, as an anonymous voice in the crowd points out, we have always been helpless against the viper as well.

"The Old Fish will save us!" someone shouts.

"Yes, the Old Fish!"

"Save us, Old Fish!"

Within seconds, the Old Fish is elected president, king and congeressman. He is still being unanimously elected to a variety of offices when he protests.

"Calm down," he orders. "Have you lost your wits? I am but a fish; I cannot stop the Red Tide."

"You defeated the viper!"

"The viper is but a fish."

"I move the Old Fish be elected apex predator!"

"I second the motion," says a tiny seahorse, glancing back over each shoulder, "but will speedily defer to any orca that might object."

"I elect the Old Fish Neptune's voice!"

"Second."

"I propose the Old Fish be elected gravity!"

"Second."

"Brothers, this is insanity. We do not even know that Red Tide will ever get here. One wind shift and it is irrelevant."

"A steady wind and we are dead!"

An aged mako emerges from the mob. I recognize her as a friend, one we swam with once, and have since passed in open waters countless times. "Old Fish," she implores, "you can do it. We believe in you."

"Even the biggest and strongest fish is still but a fish," the Old Fish answers. "I wish I could do as you ask. It is my life at risk too."

"Try," the mako pleads. "If you are right, we will all die, as we will do if you refuse to try. But if you are wrong—"

"I cannot be wrong."

The mako pauses. There is genuine wonder on her face.

"If you believe that, then how can you be but a fish?"

The Old Fish sighs and looks to me. I nod. The mako is right. If anyone can save us, it is the Old Fish.

He turns to the hammerheads. "How much time do we have?"

"Two weeks if the winds stay low."

"I would not know where to begin."

"You must begin by going to Atlantis, to consult with the Great Spotted Dolphins." I see the Old Fish's gills flare at the mention of Atlantis, and wonder why that would cause him stress. "You can make it there in four days," the mako continues, "five to return against the current. Let us pray the winds stay low."

The Old Fish notices Jotaro and shakes his head. "I am sorry, but I cannot go. This young marlin is my responsibility. I cannot abandon him, and he cannot make Atlantis in four days with an egg under his fin."

"We will care for the young marlin while you are gone."

"No. He is my responsibility, not yours."

"Then he will accompany you, and leave the egg here under our care."

"The egg stays with me," Jotaro declares.

"The boy is right," the Old Fish says. "The egg is his charge and he is mine."

"I am not your charge," Jotaro continues. "And I care nothing for all of you who come here to cheer and shout over the death of my mother."

But the thousands of fish gathered are adamant. As for me, I do not wish to see the Old Fish lose the chance to achieve his dream of Atlantis, regardless of whether the Red Tide would ever actually make it as far as the Gulf.

I call Jotaro aside. "Twenty million fish died in the last Red Tide. Do you truly believe you and the egg can survive twenty million enemies?"

He turns to the crowd and listens to their angry grumbling. He returns their hard stares. Finally, he sighs and turns the egg over to them.

"You needn't do that, Jotaro," the Old Fish protests.

I am taken aback. "Old Fish, what are you saying? The egg will be fine; you know that." He glances at me briefly, then quickly away. "Come," I say, sucking to his flank. "We have to hurry."

Within moments, we are on our way to Atlantis. Schools of fish part down the middle and we swim through, past a wake of traditional farewells.

"Swim with the current, my friends," they call after us.

"Swim with the current," we answer.

CHAPTER TWO

W HO ARE THESE dolphins we are traveling so far to see?" Jotaro asks as we near the shallow waters northeast of Havana. These are the first words he has spoken since being forced to swim with us to Atlantis, and the words are not so much spoken as spat.

Still, the Old Fish answers not with his spear, but with his heart. He has been compassionate toward Jotaro since we set off hours ago. In fact, it occurs to me that the Old Fish himself has been rather subdued, especially for one about to realize a lifelong dream.

"When the seafloor spread long ago," the Old Fish explains as he swims, "the supercontinental plate, Pangea, split into fragments. The seven fragments rafted for a time, eventually settling where they now lie. But one day, the Atlantis fragment mysteriously lost its buoyancy and sank into the sea. The humans cried, for the people of Atlantis were a beautiful, enlightened race. Their civilization was peaceful and prosperous. There was not a single law in Atlantis, because the core of every Atlantian was so pure that wrongdoing held no benefit for them.

"But the sinking of Atlantis was no accident. It was the choice of the Atlantians, whose culture was too graceful for them to continue to exist as humans. Though they needed no laws, they still needed an army, and to them, this was a misery. They tried to teach their ways to the other humans but were told that they were dreamers, and would be better served to accept reality. As their isolation increased, they grew more despondent. Finally, they decided to return to the sea, where mankind first lived. To preserve the culture they cherished, they reincarnated themselves as spotted dolphins, and sounded. The humans' loss was our gain. The wisdom of the Great Spotted Dolphins is unique, because only they have lived in the world on both sides of the sea, and know both elements: water and air. This is why we seek them."

When the Old Fish finishes, Jotaro stares at him for a long moment, then leaps high into the air, landing with a splash. "I too have long yearned to know the air," he says.

"Yes? Why is that?"

Jotaro's eyes sparkle. "Speed," he says. "The water, curse its drag, it slows me down."

The Old Fish suppresses a smile. "You would swim faster in air?"

"Use your head Old Fish. What does drag do?"

"Drags?"

"Exactly. Water is eight hundred times denser than air. Ah, how I could swim without that cursed drag."

My eyes privately meet those of the Old Fish. We remember a time when such words came from the mouth of the Old Fish himself, before he realized the principles of displacement that would render his fins useless in the air. We had tested the theory by baiting a man-of-war bird to dive after me, then trapped him to see if his wings would help him swim. The bird's clumsiness encouraged us to test the same theory with a human. When we could not find one, we enlisted the help of our friend, the mako, who dragged one from the beach for us to observe. Though it proved our theory, it was a bit of a fiasco. This is something I have never been able to understand: Every day the humans are out on the water trying to drag us out of our world and into theirs, but let one of us drag just one of them into our world—for the furtherance of science, no less—and they take it so personally. We had to swim with the mako for weeks to keep watch for all the humans hunting her.

Though it was speed that first drew the Old Fish to the air, it is the dream of the jump itself that he seeks now—to live in his dream, in the higher place, and not come crashing back down to water after a fleeting glimpse. I silently bless the distant Red Tide that has opened our dream to us.

It is still early morning when Jotaro shouts, "Food!" and whips his small frame up ninety degrees to charge a sardine that is suspended vertically in the dark blue water.

Before Jotaro can grab for it, the Old Fish thumps him away from the baited hook.

"It's mine," Jotaro wails. "I saw it first."

"Tell me Jotaro," the Old Fish says, "do you often come upon such cooperative sardines, that they so patiently await your arrival?"

He shows the young fool the fishing line, thick as sea anemone, attached to the sardine but camouflaged by the plankton-saturated water. They ascend further and the Old Fish points out the purple stick bobbing along the surface, attached to the line. Above the sea-ceiling, a black man-of-war bird hovers, its wings motionless. The Old Fish explains how they give away our location to fishermen, and how such birds are thus the mortal enemies of all fish. We sound again through the water and return to the sardine. From up close, Jotaro can now see the sharp, silver hook that has been driven through the sardine's eyes. "Sardines love to play near the shore," laments the Old Fish. "It is funny until someone loses an eye."

"How will I know which fish have pointy innards like this?" Jotaro asks.

"The dead, vertical ones might be a good place to start," I smirk.

The Old Fish laughs at my joke, and we swim on. But Jotaro's gaffe has reminded us of our hunger.

"What shall we hunt today?" the Old Fish asks.

"I see some jellyfish on the surface," I suggest.

"Ninety-nine percent water," he dismisses.

Sometimes I think the Old Fish must consider me an idiot. "Not the jellyfish, Old Fish, the man-of-war fish that swim within its tentacles."

"And how do you propose we get to them without being stung?"

Sometimes I think I must be an idiot. To save face, I joke, "Why not let Jotaro hunt them? He likes surprises."

"Clam up, marlinsucker," he snaps. "I've hunted more than you."

"How would you like me to suck your eye out of your head, you little—"

"Winkles and whelks, boys," the Old Fish exclaims. "Behave yourselves so I can concentrate, otherwise none of us will eat today."

"I do not need you to hunt for me, old-timer," Jotaro snaps. "My spear is short but swift."

I look to the surface and see the floating green Sargasso weed. "Why don't I check the Sargasso for shrimp?"

"Too small."

"There are some tattlers," I point out.

"I hate tattler," complains Jotaro.

"No one likes a tattler," I scold. "But they're filling."

The Old Fish ignores this.

"Unicornfish?"

"Pass."

"Pimpled lumpsucker?"

"Unappealing."

"Barfin goby?"

"He's ruining my appetite," Jotaro whines.

"Latin grunt?"

"What is that, a dance?"

"Pallid goby?"

The Old Fish turns to Jotaro. "That is a barfin goby an hour later." The boy giggles and I am starting to hate him.

"Why don't we sound and try to find some flounder?"

"You never eat flounder," the Old Fish says.

"I'd be willing to try it."

"Why?"

"Just for the halibut."

Some enjoy my jokes and many are pained by them, *la vida es así*. Jotaro and the Old Fish look at me and shake their heads.

"If I could help myself, I would," I say in my own defense.

Without a word, they dive deeper and I follow. As we pass Free Basin, the Old Fish brakes abruptly, and floats as still as a whale washed ashore. His eyes twinkle as he hears the distant clues. "Do you hear it?" he asks.

"Let me guess: tuna?"

"An enormous school."

Sure enough, a school of albacore tuna, with their silver sides and pretty blue backs, come into view as we lay low.

"You two stay clear," the Old Fish whispers.

Jotaro's greedy eyes are wide and his mouth trembling. "I will hunt for myself," he insists.

"These are tuna. They are very hard to hunt."

Jotaro waves him off.

"Your mother has let you hunt tuna?"

"A hundred times."

As the school nears, it is even bigger than we had hoped. Thirty feet deep and forty feet long, stuffed to the gills with tuna, who swim layered so close together they seem like one giant fish.

"A moveable feast," Jotaro marvels.

"Such a shame, how overcrowded schools are getting," I add.

"Jotaro, please stay here," the Old Fish says, his eyes never leaving the school.

"Why? They are neither dead nor vertical. Jotaro is no longer such a laughable fool."

"*Alabao*," the Old Fish sighs unhappily. "Fine, do as you wish, but stay far from my spear. This much is not for debate."

The Old Fish surges with his tail so powerfully that I feel the billow lift the rear of my body, separating me from him as he readies to attack. But before he can, we see a tuna lurch at a baited fish hanging dead and vertical in the water. The eyes of the Old Fish dart upward, and he sees the fisherman's line, and above that, the traitorous man-of-war bird splashing.

The school scatters as the Old Fish swears, "*Agua mala!* Fisherman, hunt your own!"

Just then, Jotaro explodes in pursuit. He is young, fast, and irretrievably stupid. I watch delightedly as Jotaro, rather than swipe broadside at the tuna, actually impales one on his spear. I admire his athleticism, and look forward to the moment he realizes that he has no hands with which to remove the catch.

He swims slowly back toward me and the Old Fish, as we are somersaulting with laughter. His silver cheeks are flushed, his eyes furious, humiliated. I do believe, should a thought ever venture into the virgin reef that is Jotaro's head, it would topple him over.

As the school disappears from sight, the Old Fish tries to contain his laughter, but every glance at Jotaro, hovering sullenly in front of us with a tuna nailed to his face, sends him reeling again.

"Now that's a marlinsucker!" I cry. I do not recall ever being so happy, and nicknames are racing through my mind. Note to self: Invent the camera.

Clenching his jaws in vain, the Old Fish tries to comfort Jotaro. "*Ya pasó, niño. Ya pasó.*"

"Well," I put in, "at least I'm not the only fish he bores."

"Enough Fishmael," the Old Fish scolds, then turns back to the boy. "Jotaro, Jotaro, do you see the problem here?"

"Am I stupid?" comes the muffled reply from beneath the tuna. "Yes, I see. Why have I no arms?"

"Tuna *ajoure*," I persist. "A little *avant-garde*, but I've seen it work."

"Fishmael, enough! Jotaro, fish said their farewell to arms long, long ago." To my delight, the Old Fish calmly begins to eat off Jotaro's nose as he speaks. "This is the holiness of fish, that we have no arms with which to hold on to anything. We submit to the current because we know the futility of holding on. Letting go is our way." Jotaro's face contorts as the Old Fish tears off a stubborn piece of flesh.

I am moved whenever I hear the Old Fish speak of letting go, for I remember the day he learned the lesson. Migdalia always warned him that he was too protective of her, that he lived too deeply in fear of losing her. She would say that if he lives each day in fear of the future, all he is protecting is a miserable present and besides, whenever love ends is always too soon. And he would ask, "What choice do I have?" And she would answer, "Let go. Breathe. Accept the chaos of the sea and find happiness within it. Disaster can strike at any time. To worry is to listen for the echo of a scream that has not come."

The fisherman's skiff starts to row away with its catch. "Come," says the Old Fish, "let us follow him. See how he paddles furiously with his puny oars? Such is the will of humans, their greatest strength and greatest frailty. Our Gulf Stream is a fifty-mile-wide jet stream, flowing seven hundred million gallons of water every second, yet he thinks he can challenge it. This is why you were not given hands, Jotaro, but beautiful, pliant fins."

Jotaro emerges from his embarrassment for a moment and looks up at the skiff. "He is awkward."

"He does not belong here."

"So why does he come?"

"Because God erred."

"The hands?"

"No, the brains. God gave humans too much brain. It makes them unable to accept their current. More, different and now—that is their credo." The Old Fish removes the last of the tuna and spits it toward me. I gobble it down before Jotaro can object.

He frowns. "What makes you such an expert on humans?"

The drifting shadow of the skiff envelops the Old Fish, clouding the color of his lavender sides and blue head. He glances up at the boat and sighs. For a moment, it is many years ago. The bottom of the skiff we are following is identical to the one that took Migdalia. "To survive," the Old Fish says softly, "one must know one's predators. The human predator stole my love many years ago."

"Hooked?"

The Old Fish nods ever so slightly.

"Could you not have saved her?"

Now the boy has ventured too deep and the anger of the Old Fish flashes. "Could you have saved your mother?"

But Jotaro is too naive to take offense. After a moment of thought, he replies simply, "I guess so, had I truly wanted to."

The honesty of youth paralyzes me. What Jotaro accepts as fact is a doubt that the Old Fish has dragged for years through the sea and has still never resolved. Though he would not admit it, the Old Fish has never forgiven himself for failing to beat Migdalia to *El Campeón's* hook. Migdalia's beauty was sublime, but her speed did not compare to his. And somewhere in an unexplored, aphotic zone of his heart, the Old Fish must sense that he could have taken that hook himself. A moment of hesitation, a flicker of doubt—a hero or a coward. He has never said so, but one night, as we swam a tranquil sea, he turned to me and asked, "Why is it, Fishmael, that in the moment of truth, we always fail to live up to the fish we know we can be?"

Sadly, all of our deepest held faiths are noumenons, good and bad.

"Pay the boy no attention," I interject, "he cannot even tell bait from food."

"Oh can't I?" Jotaro huffs.

Before I can answer, a sandy voice penetrates the sea-ceiling from above. It is a silent, windless morning. The voice is clear but distant, as though calling into a cavern.

"If the others heard me talking out loud," it says, *"they would think that I am crazy. But since I am not crazy, I do not care. And the rich have radios to talk to them in their boats and to bring them baseball."*

"Who is he talking to?" I ask.

The Old Fish shrugs, looking toward the bottom of the skiff in wonder. "What is baseball?"

"What is rich?"

We wait for more, but hear only the screech of a man-of-war bird. I notice the child prodigy sound into cold, dark water. There is another baited hook down there, but I do not bother to stop him. The truth is, I am tiring of him, and would consider our pilgrimage none the worse for his absence. Should his past embarrassment lead him into poor judgment now, it is not my problem. Let him drag his failures through the sea with him the rest of his life. I don't care.

As the Old Fish awaits another word from the human, Jotaro nibbles at the baited sardine below. My contempt for him dissolves into admiration as I watch him; clearly he has learned something, and is trying to pick off the sardine gently to see what is baited beneath it. It is a good plan. He does not wish to play another round of winner take nothing.

"Yes! Yes!" comes the sandy voice from the other side, as Jotaro tugs ever so slightly at the sardine. The fisherman's rowing oars disappear from the water.

The Old Fish hears the bloodlust of the fisherman. He sees the purple stick at the surface dip sharply. Quickly, he realizes what is happening. Again, the man-of-war bird shrieks its call. Again, the purple stick bobs in the water. Down below, Jotaro is struggling to remove the sardine's head without stabbing himself. The Old Fish spins and charges Jotaro, as the voice continues.

"*Come on, make another turn. Just smell them. Aren't they lovely? Eat them good now and then there is the tuna. Hard and cold and lovely. Don't be shy, fish. Eat them.*"

Down below, the Old Fish swipes his tail to thump Jotaro away from the danger, but Jotaro has learned this too, and he sideswims the attack. The current caused by the swipe pitches Jotaro to his left, just as he is about to grab for the exposed tuna. His anal fin brushes against the bait, pushing it off to the right.

"*He'll take it. God help him to take it.*"

Now the two marlins roll over each other, Jotaro trying to dodge the Old Fish and the Old Fish trying to block Jotaro's path. Jotaro slashes his tiny spear at the Old Fish, who accepts the blow to the side of his head rather than elude the attack and clear Jotaro's way to the bait. I feel a pang of guilt for having teased the boy. Still, I am hoping he wins and gets what he wants.

"*He can't have gone,*" comes the evil prayer of the human. "*Christ knows he can't have gone.*"

With an acceleration that chills my blood, Jotaro dashes around the Old Fish and bursts downward a fathom toward the bait. His mouth touches the tuna. The Old Fish spins and I catch a glimpse of his great eye.

The past shines in it.

Jotaro dissolves and Migdalia returns. Once again she is reaching for *El Campeón's* hook. The Old Fish swims in delirious pursuit of the fish he yearns to be. There is history and anguish and punishment and joy in the eye of the Old Fish as he descends.

"No!" I scream, but I am too late.

The Old Fish overwhelms Jotaro and seizes the bait away from the boy in a decisive chomp. In his wake, I am stunned. I would sooner believe that the sea had really frozen into the solid block of ice it feels like right now.

But the Old Fish does not fight his downward momentum. I follow him. At one hundred fifty fathoms, his body levels, and he continues swimming within the northeastern current. He slows enough for me to catch up, and the sight of my magnificent teacher gouged through the mouth like a common tuna is more than I can bear. It is unthinkable, made nonetheless so by the triviality of having seen it happen.

"Old Fish, you're hooked. How can this be?"

He does not answer me. His eyes are distant, unmoved. I assume he is in shock. He stares straight ahead as he swims, steady and unconcerned, as though nothing has happened. I scurry to his face and stare into the faraway eye.

"Old Fish," I plead, "we must sound. Go as deep as possible, snap this piddling line."

He ignores me. Jotaro swims within range and yells down bitterly, "Swim with the current old-timer, if you can," before swimming away. I would kill the boy if I could, but the Old Fish merely glances up toward him and continues swimming. Seeing his eye move, I realize that he is not in shock at all. Indeed, he is not even upset. If there is any name for his aspect at all, it is gratitude. The Old Fish has not just lost; he has won.

Jotaro's ignorance has afforded the Old Fish the opportunity to right the past and accept the punishment he has long sought. His oblation to Migdalia.

Stoically, he moves forward. From above, the fisherman shouts, *"Now!"* and the line is jerked fiercely, gashing the metal hook into the flesh of the Old Fish and lodging it in the right side of his mouth. I see the protruding point of the hook tear a ragged line from his mouth to his jaw. Again and again the line is jerked and with each pull, the Old Fish's body contorts in pain as the hook digs deeper into him. It is blasphemy. It seems to go on forever.

When the fisherman finally stops, the Old Fish and I both breathe in gasps. The hook is a gruesome sight, desecrating the wise and beautiful old face. A sheath of muscle oozes from the wound, raw and throbbing.

The Old Fish shudders under the pain but continues to swim, as if by inertia alone. His eyes have returned to the present. For the first time ever, I see fear in them.

CHAPTER THREE

WE SWIM IN silence, gradually making our way back toward the thermocline. The midday sun makes it a clean, well-lighted place, and fish pass by quietly, taking little notice of our plight. No suffering is so profound that it cannot be ignored. I suction to the Old Fish's belly to steady my nerves. So many years. So many wars. We had learned the depths to remove chaos from the sea, only to fall to the heartless order of the world above. We are hooked. I say it over and over again and still, I cannot believe it. I begin to say it aloud like a chant, half expecting the Old Fish to disagree, to explain to me why this is not the end. How can this be the end? It is not possible. Not now, not when we are finally about to achieve Atlantis. Then again, does anyone recognize his own end before the final crossing? Or is it just another shift in current, easy to feel but hard to admit?

"We are hooked," I repeat.

"You are not hooked," comes the soothing voice of the Old Fish. His manner is calm, almost relieved, and for a moment I am hopeful. "You are freer than you know, Fishmael. All that will change for you is that you will need to find another home."

I wince. The notion is obscene. I would rather be dead; it's just that I don't want to die.

"Old Fish, please," I say, glad that he is finally speaking again. "We must sound. We're in deep enough waters. We'll dive at full speed and take the slack out of the line. It'll snap; I know it."

He shakes his head slowly, side to side. "I have always trusted my current. Now, this is my current."

"It is an interruption of your current."

"Perhaps. It is always hard to say."

"What about your dream of Atlantis?"

"Perhaps another year."

"There are no other years if we do not escape this hook!"

"I have seen many fish swimming free with hooks still in their mouths. Not all fishermen want to kill. Not all are *El Campeón*."

"You cannot bring Migdalia back, Old Fish."

His eye barely moves, but rebukes me as severely as would his spear. I should have known better. Friendship is leeway, not complete freedom. When a friend sees too deeply, the friendship must either grow or die. I fall silent, wondering which it will be for us.

A strange fish approaches awkwardly, nearly swimming right into the Old Fish. It is small, round and flat, and apparently blind. We are not a difficult pair to see, the Old Fish and I. I wonder how this little fish ever managed to survive as long as he has, with such poor instincts. But as the fish turns, I see his problem: Both of his eyes are on the right side of his head. This does not bode well for a long, pelagic life.

Flounder and sole have eyes on only one side of their heads, but are wise enough to spend their lives on the seabed, optic side up. I have heard that humans too suffer this design defect. I assume the land must be safer than the sea, or surely they would have evolved by now.

This is no flounder which has bumbled into us, however, and it is not a species of sole indigenous to these waters either. But sole are notorious for their poor sense of direction, which is why so many of them get lost. As the fish turns to see us, he notices the spear of the Old Fish and follows its full length in awe before reaching his face. The fish withdraws a bit, cautious, but not exactly afraid.

The Old Fish leans his spear far away from the little fish. "Do not worry," he says. "I will do you no harm."

"Do as you wish," the fish answers, to my surprise. "I don't care."

He begins scanning his surroundings, barely paying attention to us.

"You are a fringed sole, are you not?" the Old Fish asks.

"I'm sorry, did you say something?"

"Are you a fringed sole?"

"Yes."

"What are you doing in the Gulf? These are not your waters. Are you lost?"

Again the small fish has forgotten about our presence. "What? I'm sorry, were you still talking?"

"Are you lost?"

"No," he answers absently. "No, I cannot help you. I am lost myself. My entire school perished in the Red Tide off Africa. I have been swimming north since then. Is this the Arabian Sea?"

The Old Fish and I look at each other. "It is the Gulf Stream," I say.

"Gulf Stream? What Gulf?"

"Mexico."

He absorbs the news slowly. "Mexico? These are not my waters."

"Now that you mention it."

He becomes agitated. "What am I doing here? You must lead me to the Arabian Sea," he demands. "Come, we'll retrace my path."

The Old Fish and I look again at each other. Apparently, the silver hook sticking out of the Old Fish's face is too subtle for the sole.

"Our time is kind of committed right now," I say, motioning to the hook.

"Committed?"

"We're with a friend."

"Did you know you're hooked?" the lost sole says suddenly, noticing the line. "I once heard it doesn't hurt. Does it hurt?"

I have rarely seen the Old Fish run thin on patience. "It is a hook," he says. "It is sharp, it is steel, and it is going—as you can see—through my face. Use your imagination."

The fish does not hear any of this, just swims away, still muttering about the Arabian Sea.

"Poor fish," the Old Fish says as we watch it leave. His gills flare as he sighs deeply.

"Yes, but Old Fish, do you hear what I hear?"

"What is that, Fishmael?"

"It is your current. It has just shifted again."

"What are you saying?"

"In my entire life, I have never before seen a fish looking for the Arabian Sea in the Gulf Stream. His visit was no accident."

"No?"

"No. It was three currents that brought him here. The Benguela Current, the Florida Current and your current."

"Fishmael . . ."

"If you trust the currents, you trust them always. A fish appears just when you are ready to surrender your life, and reminds us of why we are making pilgrimage to Atlantis in the first place."

A light spreads across the face of the Old Fish. "The Red Tide," he realizes.

"The Red Tide," I repeat. "Your sworn responsibility to the sea. Even if your dream of Atlantis means nothing to you, surely twenty million fish awaiting your return do."

"The Red Tide. You are a wise little sucker, Fishmael. You have seen a current that I missed. We must escape this wretched hook so that we can save the sea."

A current is an elusive thing. Just as the oceanic currents that surround us, it can be felt if one knows how. But the currents of the ocean are easy to feel. A fish simply stops swimming, stops talking, stops listening and stops trying, and the current reveals itself. The process is the same for one's inner current, but the results are unpredictable. Preconceptions are harder to stop than swimming, talking, listening and trying, and too often, our true current remains a mystery.

I watch as the Old Fish again shifts his current. For now, I do not care whether the new current is real or imagined. I want to save our lives. He begins whipping his blue head back and forth, trying to dislodge the hook, stopping abruptly when the pain becomes too much. His eyes are active, his gills flaring and closing. The hook is no longer a victory. A second time, he bears up beneath his pain and thrashes wildly, battering the fishing line with his spear. There is great suffering in his eyes. Once again, the hook refuses to dislodge.

I rush to his head and throw my meaningless weight against the line. It is no use; I might as well be trying to tear a conger eel in half. The Old Fish vomits his stomach and the full, salmon pink length of it comes out through his mouth. But the hook is in his mouth, not in his stomach, and the good idea comes to nothing. The stomach retracts into his abdomen. A third time now, the Old Fish braces himself and flails at the line. A third time, his will is overcome by his pain, and he is still. His entire body trembling now, he tries to calm himself and think. Never has he met with a foe he could not defeat, but this fishing line is unwilling to fight back.

Finally, he looks at me. "What can I do?" he asks.

I brush myself across his anguished nape to comfort him. I feel so helpless. If he cannot defeat the line, how can I? Again, his gills flare and I want to duck into them and wait while he delivers another victory to us. But I know that this is not a luxury I have today. "Sound, Old Fish," I implore. "Sound and snap the line."

But the torrent of his panic is gaining speed, his head swimming in white water. The words pour from his mouth fast and fitfully.

"What if the line is stronger than I? It could tear the hook through my jaw and leave me to die all the same. Or it could hold but injure me worse, leaving me in the depths and unable to defend myself."

"Then jump. Perhaps the hook will come loose."

"But if I jump, the air bladders in my belly will fill with air, keeping me nearer to the fisherman. He might have a gaff like the one *El Campeón* drove into Migdalia. Perhaps it is a hundred men aboard the boat. Young, fierce, well-fed, fish-hating men with arms as thick as my trunk, taking turns at the line to stay fresh.

Oh, Fishmael, why did you have to tease Jotaro? . . ." His voice trails off.

Startled by the accusation, I begin to respond. But seeing the way he holds his addled stare on me, I know this is not the time for it. "We have to do something," I say, but he does not answer, and I know that for the first time in our lives, he is depending on me for a solution. He is too honorable to say that I owe him, but I know what he is thinking. And he is right, of course. All our lives, he has defended us, hunted for us and even swam for us. Who am I to fail him now, when he finally needs me?

If the universe holds a more tender bond than guardian and guarded, I do not know it. I would die quickly out here without my friend, it's true, but the Old Fish has needs too. There is no creature more alone than a savior with no one to save, like the parent of no children.

An idea springs to mind. "Let's ask the Great Spotted Dolphins!" I exclaim.

"We are still far. I do no know if I can drag the boat all the way to Atlantis. It might be an enormous boat."

"We have seen the bottom of the boat. It is small. Just a skiff, smaller than you."

"Still, to drag it all the way to Atlantis?"

"Then there must be someone else we can consult. Someone who is wise. How about the Hardheaded Catfish?"

The Old Fish allows the slightest wisp of hope to cross his face. During our years in the depths, we had heard talk of the Hardheaded Catfish of *Sagua la Grande*. It was said that he had answers. That he had studied the Spotted Dolphins and sent turtles on land to observe the humans and report back to him. I remember wondering how turtles—hard of hearing and slow afoot—ever got close enough to the humans to learn from them. The answer to my question will come soon.

THE SEABED NEAR *Sagua la Grande* is shallow and soon it is in sight. In my enthusiasm, I flash ahead of the Old Fish, my body nearly vertical, my eyes darting right to left in search of the Hardheaded Catfish. Behind me, the Old Fish moves cautiously. The hook is hurting him, flaunting its power over him with every move he makes. I circle back and sidle to his keel, and we continue our descent patiently, careful not to lodge the hook any deeper or make the line any tighter.

The beauty of *Sagua la Grande* is so enchanting that I am tempted to enjoy it, almost forgetting why we have come. Its seabed needs no markings to announce it; one always knows when he is passing over *Sagua la Grande*. The flora is its signature, a lush cascade of color that coddles the neon blennies and gobies who burrow into its roots and dine on the nutrients of its coral reef. Blushing crimson and flushed orange bouquets of sea anemone glimmer like orichalc, and the entire seabed seems to dance for us in the under flow.

The light fades only slightly as we descend, and a

chill tinges the water. We level ourselves to drift as we survey the area in search of the catfish. The water is always calmer below, and if not for the predators, I would quite like it here. The surface is all flash and crash that achieves nothing; the only true movement of water lies in the deep currents, invisible to the eye. There are even invisible waves down here, wherever waters of different densities meet. I wonder if the fish of the deep have ever seen a surface wave. I wonder if I will ever see a sky wave. I wonder if the human has waves beyond his comprehension that are moving the waters of his life. I am acutely aware of my own ignorance. I must be, so often does the sea prove it to me.

At a clearing, I see a batfish waddling foolishly along the seabed, using her fins to walk instead of swim. I point her out to the Old Fish and we share a light moment. A bit farther, the floor falls off into a deep chasm. Through the shadows, we see movement. We move closer. There seems to be something that looks like a very large catfish lying on the sandy bottom of the fissure. It is hard to be sure through the cloud of sand circling slowly above it, but it is gray and scavenging the floor.

The Old Fish cannot fit through the split rock, so I go on alone the last few fathoms. Alas, on approach, I am disappointed to find that it is only a nurse shark. Nurse sharks, like catfish, spend their lives on the seabed, sifting through the sand for food. They rarely travel, and see little of the world. But such is their current. So designed for laziness are they, that they are one of the few species of shark that need not swim in order to breathe.

"What do you want?" the nurse shark demands when she sees me. I have disturbed her hunt.

"I'm looking for a Hardheaded Catfish," I answer, glancing back to be sure the Old Fish is near.

The shark rubs the area where her chin might be. "I know a lot of fancy mantas. People who can guide you out of the flora."

"They move smooth," I defer, "but have no answers."

"That depends. Why'd you come here?" she asks, regarding me suspiciously through her small, yellow slit eyes.

"I serve the Old Fish," I explain.

"It is not wise to serve old fish."

This is a bad sign. She has never heard of us, which will make the rest of my explanation harder. Indicating the giant marlin hovering above us, I explain how we have been charged with saving the sea from the approaching Red Tide, and that if we cannot free ourselves from the hook, we cannot solicit the advice of the Great Spotted Dolphins of Atlantis. I speak beautifully, persuasively. We need her help, I say. She does not respond—simply eyes me, trying to decide if I am worth her time. During the lull, I decide on impulse to describe our lifelong dream of Atlantis and the sky, hoping it will help to convince her. But my words bring only a sneer to her mouth.

"That is a foolish dream," she scoffs at length. "There is no such thing as sky. There is sand and there are scraps of food. Now go away. I know of no Hard-headed Catfish. Swim with the current."

"Swim with the current," I answer dejectedly, and begin to rise out of her abyss.

But the Old Fish comes to the mouth of the crevice and calls down, "Fishmael, did you explain to the good shark that she too will die if we cannot stop the Red Tide?"

The shark's eyes widen. "Beg pardon?" she asks. "What's that word he just used?"

"The one he used just now?" I ask.

"Yes, that's the one."

"The one meant to describe your own, personal and very specific fate in the event you don't help us?" She nods. "Yes, that was, *die*." I punctuate the word crisply, causing her to flinch.

"Oh," she clarifies with convenient speed, "Hard-headed *Cat*fish. I thought you said 'gelatinous seasnail.' Of course. Follow me. I'll lead you to him."

The catfish resides beneath a rocky ledge in the deepest section of the *Sagua la Grande* Basin. The ledge is so surrounded by cones and ridges that, without the help of the nurse shark, we never would have found it.

It is said that, though he rarely leaves his cove, the catfish sees all. Fish come from far, wide and deep to see him, to feed on his wisdom. For years, says the nurse shark, he turned all away, unable to spare the time away from his work. But recently, a catfish envoy announced that the Hardheaded Catfish had unlocked the infinite mystery of the time-matter-energy complex of the universe and its implications for biomass everywhere, and so he had some free time before his next project. Selected visitors would be welcome for a limited time only.

"Apparently," the shark confides, "humans are very interested in something they call nuclear fishin'. As his next sacred task, the catfish will find out where the nuclear live and warn them."

With that, she leaves us, asking that we not mention to the catfish that it was she who advised us of his whereabouts. She is not confident enough of our worthiness to risk his wrath; she has a hunch that this fishin' involves an especially succulent breed of mollusk.

As we wedge ourselves beneath the ledge into the dark cove, I am stunned by the opulence. Translucent mother-of-pearl shells cover the rock walls and chime with every wave that passes through. A canopy of sundown yellow orichalc hangs above us, glittering like the sea at midday. Sergeant major fish line the arches of doorways built of coral, their bright yellow backs reflecting an amber glow. Each passageway is guarded by dozens of night sergeants. The Old Fish and I smile at one another and nod.

"Halt!" shouts a night sergeant upon our approach. "If you wish to enter this holy place, you must first swear to obey the rules."

"We swear," I say quickly.

"Good," the pale, striped fish says. "Kiss the doorway." We comply with his strange request but it only leads to another. "Touch your foreheads to the dirt."

Again we obey, though the Old Fish is forced to invert his entire body in the narrow space, to maneuver around his spear. "Now wrap this seaweed around your head and chew on this shell. Excellent. Now announce yourselves."

After introducing ourselves and explaining our situation, we are led by another night sergeant into a dark inner chamber and instructed to remain silent. The Hardheaded Catfish is in consultation with a turtle and cannot be disturbed.

"Is it one of the turtles that went on land to research the humans for him?" I ask.

"No," answers the night sergeant, "merely a disillusioned loggerhead. The catfish will acknowledge you once he is through. Until then, remain still and silent."

With that he leaves us. We can hear the conversation from where we wait, but are careful not to disturb it. The Old Fish is nearly immobilized by the snag of the fishing line on a sharp edge of coral. He holds still so as not to chip the coral or create any disruption.

Through the shadows we see the brown catfish hovering before a large loggerhead turtle. The catfish is smaller than I expected, much smaller than I. He listens patiently to the giant turtle as it speaks in a voice full of dismay, its eyes cast downward.

"I have come to you to ask you to teach me the ten concentric circles of life," the turtle says.

"Circles?" the catfish asks with amusement.

"I have heard that my ancestors so revered these circles and the enlightenment they held, that they sought the most private place to chart them. It is said that they swam the expanse of the Celtic Sea to the English Channel, to The Solent north of the Isle of Wight. There they climbed onto the land and trekked for many years, until they reached an isolated place called Avebury, where—"

"Stop," the catfish commands and the turtle is immediately silent. He looks up at the catfish, shame in his eyes. "Poor, ignorant turtle," the catfish says soothingly, "hear me well. You are merely weak from lack of food."

The Old Fish and I glance sideways toward one another, neither of us willing to risk interrupting the sacred proceedings, but surprised by the catfish's quick diagnosis.

"Unworthy reptile," the catfish continues, "understand this: One plant-eater must eat ten times his body weight to live. One carnivorous shrimp must eat ten times his body weight of plant-eaters to live. What is it that you eat?"

A wave passes and the shell chimes ring softly in the outer chamber as the loggerhead curls his fore-flippers once to stay in place, sending the catfish drifting back a fathom. The catfish returns to the bulbous head of the turtle as the turtle says, "Invertebrates mostly. Some conch, crab . . ."

"Do you see the problem?" The turtle says nothing, so the catfish explains. "You are working too hard for your food," he smiles. "An orca whale eats everything! Perhaps he eats a shark which has eaten ten marlin which have eaten a hundred tuna which have eaten a thousand crabs. Why chase a thousand crabs when one orca will fill your belly with them?"

"But how am I to keep pace with an orca whale?" the turtle asks.

"You must shed your shell," the catfish proclaims. "Of course you are a slow swimmer with all that weight, that bony plastron across your chest and heavy shell on your back."

"But these are my protection," protests the turtle.

"Nonsense," replies the catfish, "they are your burden. See my acolytes outside and they will remove your shell. Trust me, then swim with the current, my magnificent friend! I have spoken."

The turtle hurries past the Old Fish and me, excited to begin his new life.

"Did he just tell the turtle to discard his shell and start hunting killer whales?" I whisper to the Old Fish.

But before the Old Fish can answer, the catfish bellows, "Next!"

Cautiously, we approach. From here, I can see him much better. His brow is wrinkled in a perpetual furrow, and his eyes are glassy and certain.

"Learned catfish," the Old Fish asks, "will the turtle not be killed and eaten by the first orca he attacks?"

"He will be fine, my friend," the catfish assures us.

"But—"

"Oh, what a curse, my profundity," the catfish sighs to himself. "How much deeper must I go, to avoid those who cannot see the truth?"

"We wish to see," I say eagerly, taking a single stroke toward him. He halts me sternly.

"Stop," he demands, brushing his mustache against the rock. "Have my guards explained to you the rules of conduct in my home?"

"They have," says the Old Fish, "but I must admit, I am unfamiliar with them."

"Yes," he nods patiently, "of course you are. As are all fish . . . for now."

"So it is true, what we have heard?" the Old Fish asks. "Have you really sent turtles on land to learn the ways of the humans?" The catfish merely nods. "And their poor hearing was not an impediment?"

"There are no impediments," the catfish says with eyes wide. He lashes his tail and swims up the nape of the Old Fish, speaking directly to his right eye. "I have learned their religions. The secret to all things. Did they tell you outside about the time-matter-energy complex?"

"Yes, they did," the Old Fish answers. "Congratulations on that. But actually," he adds almost apologetically, "I need only the secret to a rather simple thing."

"What is that, my friend?"

"How do I get this hook out of my face?"

The catfish turns and rests himself on the spear of the Old Fish. Hanging his bearded head off the tip of it, he inspects the hook closely. He swims inverted along the underside of the spear to get even closer. The Old Fish opens his jaws, showing the silver metal clearly against the pale interior of his mouth.

"This the hook you're talking about?" the catfish calls.

"It is," mumbles the Old Fish.

The brown barbels of the catfish's mustache arch as he scoffs. "Easy. Just pray."

"Pray? To whom?"

"To Bob."

"Who's Bob?"

"He's the one," the catfish says. "The one the humans pray to. Anything you want, you pray to Bob for it."

We are confused. "And that helps . . . how?"

"Atheist!" the catfish accuses, pointing a fin at the Old Fish. His mustache stands on end.

"What?"

"If you do not believe," he thunders, his eyes bulging, "you will never reap the rewards."

"What rewards?"

"Anything you want! That is the majesty of Bob. He will give you anything you want if you only pray for it! So you must believe, you must!"

"Can Bob get the hook out of my face?"

"Child," the catfish sighs, "of course. He does far better things than that."

"Like what?"

The catfish cannot believe our ignorance. "Oh, for the love of Bob, children, don't you see? Anything! He can even forgive you."

"Forgive me?"

"Yes!"

"What is that? Forgive?"

"He lets you off the hook."

The Old Fish and I exhale. Finally, we're getting somewhere.

"Wonderful," says the Old Fish eagerly, "so get me off the hook."

"Okay," the catfish says, springing up again onto the spear of the Old Fish. "What bad thing did you do?"

"I ate a hook."

"That's not bad."

"It seems like a bad idea now."

"Yes, but it doesn't require forgiveness," the catfish points out.

"But you said forgiveness is letting me off the hook."

"Not that hook. The hook of doing evil things."

"I do not do evil things."

"Then you do not need forgiveness," the catfish concludes. "Bob loves you. Praised be the aim of the bored. Next!"

The Old Fish sighs deeply and looks to me.

"Catfish," I venture, "we do not understand this word, 'forgiveness.'"

"It means you can do evil things without getting in trouble, as long as you admit to Bob that you did an evil thing and ask him to forgive you."

"But there is only desire, obstacle and appetite in the sea." I paraphrase my earlier lesson. "There is no evil."

"But now there can be!" the catfish exults. "That's the genius of Bob! Do anything you want, to anyone you want, and if you tell Bob you're sorry you did it, everything's as cool as the other side of the flounder!"

The Old Fish rattles his head to clear it of the thought. "With all due respect, catfish, I have no need of such grand favors of Bob. Would you just show me how to pray to be rid of this hook?"

The catfish is disappointed by our lack of ambition, but he is eager to spread his gospel, no easy task from under a rock. "Very well," he agrees, "first close your eyes. Good. Now ask Bob to take the hook out of your mouth."

I keep one eye open as the Old Fish prays, but the hook does not move. The Old Fish continues to pray fervently, but with no success. Finally, he rests.

"It does not seem to be working," he says.

"Are you sure you're pronouncing the name right?"

"Bob," says the Old Fish.

"Yes, that's it. What about your little friend? Is he praying for the opposite?"

"No!" I shout. "Of course not."

"Because you don't want to confuse Bob."

"Certainly not," says the Old Fish.

The catfish gnaws on his moustache. "How about vomiting your stomach?"

"We tried that," I say. "It didn't work."

"Just as well," the catfish nods. "It's a vile habit."

"Maybe Bob favors men over fish," the Old Fish suggests. "After all, he is their Bob."

"Impossible," the catfish dismisses. "Bob created both fish and man. In fact, He created fish before He created man."

"Really?"

"Yes. Fish were created on the fifth day of the earth, man on the sixth, and on the seventh day, Bob rested."

Note to self: Revisit petition for five-day work week.

"Then again," the catfish considers, "maybe men are favored. When Bob flooded the earth, He promised to treat humans best and the naked man, Noah, started sacrificing animals the very next day."

"Wait a minute," I interrupt, "are you sure you don't mean *God*?"

"Who?"

"Old fish, this catfish is a fool. We know God. All creatures know God." Though we have clearly wasted time, the Old Fish is reluctant to give up on the catfish. Hope is a brutal temptress, who comes and goes and breaks your heart in both directions.

"Hardheaded Catfish, is there anything else we can try?"

The catfish is amused by our ignorance. "Poor, foolish fish, there is nothing more than Bob. All paths lead to Bob."

"Our path leads to Atlantis," I say.

"Atlantis? Why do you want to go to Atlantis?"

"To save the sea from the Red Tide," says the Old Fish.

Now the catfish is thoroughly entertained. "No marlin can save the sea," he laughs. "You swim too high. You are big and powerful and beautiful and irritating to the rest of us. The sea can only be saved from below, by me and Bob."

"But we wish to know the sky."

"The sky?" He looks at me with great pity in his eyes, stroking my head comfortingly as he continues. "Oh remora, poor ignorant fish. Sad, gray, slow-witted, flank-sucking parasite." I silently look to the Old Fish, then back to the catfish. "Lamentable, phlegmatic, cowardly, fetid feculent wretch—be realistic. There is no such thing as sky. What you feel when you jump is not real; it is just a dream."

"Our dream is real."

"The splash is real," counters the catfish. "Seafloor spreading is real. Red Tide, continental rafting and worldwide ecosystem collapse. Sand. Crushed mollusk, unattended barnacle eggs, sea lice. That is what is real. Now come, let us stop this foolish talk and pray to this glassine chunk I found amid the coral."

We excuse ourselves and leave the dark cove as the catfish inserts a sand dollar into his mouth and waits for it to melt.

SWIMMING BACK TOWARD the thermocline, we agree to head northeast while we consider our options, to stay on course for Atlantis. I regret the time wasted with the Hardheaded Catfish and his evangelical priapism. Time is too precious to be squandered searching out others with solutions to our problem. Night is laying its sapphire blanket over the sea as we reach the thermocline. The surface waters have cooled with the setting of the sun. I am still fuming.

"He had nothing to teach us," I complain.

"Except to beware of praying humans," the Old Fish notes.

"How can he know if the sky exists from such depth? I have been with you. I have seen it. It is there."

"Why did you have to antagonize Jotaro, Fishmael?"

"We do not need him."

"The boy could help. He could jump to see what we are up against. You cannot jump and I cannot afford to."

"We will attain our dream without him."

The pain is wearing on the Old Fish, and there is great sadness in his eyes when he sighs, "Perhaps the catfish is right. Perhaps it is a foolish dream."

"Old Fish, do not let your mind get away from you. The catfish was a wahoo."

"In a sea full of fish," he counters, "I have yet to hear of anyone ever learning the sky. A thousand times I have leapt, only to splash down again into the water. Never once have I stayed even a moment longer than the jump before. My dreams are unrealistic. I am the wahoo."

"You are the one who taught me to have faith in my current."

"Currents," he laughs sadly, "an invention of my mind to make sense of this wild water. How does any-one know his true current?"

As if in answer to his question, a flimsy stream of pale green liquid comes from the skiff above, cuts through the night air and punctures the water.

The Old Fish is aghast. "*Coño!* Does he urinate on us now?"

But the urine reminds me of something. I watch as it hits the water, and a gentle, circular wave spreads out around it. Concentric circles spread then fade into the sea, as the urine sinks in a cloudy swirl. The Old Fish is unwilling to look back at me as I watch him accept this newest degradation at the hands, or whatever, of the fisherman. I want to speak, but the truth catches in my throat.

There was a day though—back when the Old Fish still believed in currents, and the opinions of clever, ignorant catfish meant nothing to us—there was a day when the Old Fish taught me about the ten concentric circles of life, the secret of happiness. The secret to knowing your current.

The fish who follows his current is easy to recognize. His colors are dazzling, his eyes clear and bright. He is a joyous fish, calm and strong. He trusts his inner current as he trusts the timeless current of the ocean. He would no sooner fight the drag against his current than he would try to swim against the sea. He sees desire and appetite for the lures that they are, and is not slave to his own empty stomach.

While the rest of us thrash after our riptide dreams like hungry vipers—cursing our bad luck and weak fins when we tire, only to watch helplessly as our dreams drift ever farther into the distance—he stays true to his current. His swim is as refreshing as ours is draining. He does not chase his dreams; he allows them to pull him toward their loving embrace. Not content to make our living, we fight to make our killing, even though in the process what we are killing is ourselves. Then we look at him with bitter eyes and call him lucky. But he is not lucky, just in harmony with his inner call.

The Old Fish was once this fish.

But today, with the hook weakening his resolve, he asks, how does one know for certain the current which is his? How does he know it without doubt, for doubt is the real apex predator. Doubt is the hunter no one defeats and no one outswims. Many are they who would follow their current faithfully, if only they were sure it was the one for which they live. But the sea is a calamitous, confusing gyre, ever shifting and swelling, hatching and killing. And in the midst of all that, how is any fish to know with confidence the path which is his? How do we place faith in the invisible?

The secret to faith, the Old Fish taught me years ago, lies in the ten concentric circles unique to each fish, which reveal his true nature.

The ten concentric circles of life.

Chart your circles, he would say.

Find a safe cove, then brush the sand with your tail, fin or spear, in the design of concentric circles. With the design in front of you, close your eyes and ask yourself, what is the single thing—the single thing—without which life would be worthless. Solicit no other opinions. Reveal to no one your final decision. Simply know it quietly, yourself. That will be your innermost circle. Do not chart it as a list; the values of the heart are not linear and a list will only confuse matters.

It will not be easy. You will likely find yourself undecided between two or three values, all precious to you. At that moment, you must envision your life with only one of them, and ask hard and bare if it retains its value without the others.

Once you have chosen this core circle and are sure, ask yourself what is next closest to your heart. What is the next most important thing, that without which life is a misery. Again, there will be much that is dear to you, and to choose in linear form will not work. The only way to know is to see the circles, to imagine your life with the one and ask if it retains its value without the others. Repeat this process again and again. Stay in your cove without food or company until you have drawn ten circles in the sand.

Once you are done, admire your result. Savor it. Absorb the target in the sand before you. Imprint its message into your heart and take heed of it. For if you have been honest with yourself, when you are through, your path will appear. You will finally understand what it is you ask of this world, and therefore, in which direction you must swim to find it. You will understand why you must fail when the dreams of your eyes conflict with those of your heart. You will see the outer circles in proper context, and never again will you pursue your eighth circle at the expense of your third. It is easy to ignore those pursuits that lie outside the ten circles. The lethal temptations for all fish, however, are circles eight, nine and ten. Depending on when those are pursued, they are either benign aspirations, or the treasonous light in the maw of the viper. One must establish the concentric foundation before piling upon it. Because he who chases outer circles out of order and stacks them on a hollow core, only adds weight to that which will inevitably crumble down upon him. In other words: Do not offer to bear Neptune's carriage before you are strong enough to support it. Carry his trident; he will not kill you if you drop that.

Now, the restless ale of the sea will soon erase your chart, but the etching will remain in your heart forever, or at least until your circles change, for they are forever in flux.

For most of his life, the core circle of the Old Fish was life itself—breathing, moving and eating. For me, it was mackerel. Then we met Migdalia and the heart of the Old Fish saw everything through the tint of her love. I changed mine to balao. When Migdalia died, his core circle became hate. For me, small squid, the kind with the heads that just pop right off.

The sea is completely dark now, and in the distance, we hear the unmistakable splashing of dolphins at play. They do not notice us as they tumble past, rolling and blowing over each other. They are long gone before the Old Fish and I can take our eyes off the spot we last saw them. I know that he is thinking of the same thing as I.

I can see the Old Fish and Migdalia romping through the sea as though they were children, sure that life would last forever. I hear Migdalia's laugh, spirited to the point of indelicate. I see her vivid coloring, crisp violet stripes flecked with white spots, as soft and white as clouds. It was a cloudy day when *El Campeón* took to the sea in search of her. It was raining by the time he found her.

Suddenly, the time we had with Migdalia seems so short. I remember, as a young fish, asking her if the circles could help me find a mate for myself. After all, I said, having seen the love between her and the Old Fish, love was now my core. Despite this, my mate had failed to appear. I followed my circles faithfully, and still she did not appear. Why were the circles failing me, I asked. Why did it seem that every other fish in the sea swam with another, while I sucked onto the Old Fish alone?

"Dear Fishmael," she smiled sadly, "love is not prey; it cannot be hunted. Love is a miracle. But for the one who follows his current, it is an inevitable miracle."

I remember how her words saddened me. I felt so helpless. I wanted strokes that I could take to bring about what I wanted. But all I could do was wait for a miracle.

"So when it comes to love," I lamented with eyes closed, "the circles offer no answer."

But then she brought her face to mine and lifted me gently by her spear. "To the contrary," she smiled, "the entire answer is in the circles. He who is true to himself and his current creates an expression of himself that is his highest self—clean, proud and right. Only the best self can find the best mate, for he is the best mate. The lowest self finds the mate suited for that lowest expression, yielding a lifetime of low expression. Love is not a question of if, only of when and whom. Fishmael," she whispered, "sometimes, searching for something is the only thing that makes it lost."

No one but the Old Fish will ever know why he hesitated when Migdalia grabbed for *El Campeón's* line. Never once had she beaten the Old Fish into battle. Was it simply fear of the hook? It only takes an instant of doubt for life to change completely. In fact, I do not believe it ever changes any other way.

My belly feels as though a school of live blennies are in there. How I long to hear that indelicate laugh just once more. The Old Fish is still transfixed on the fading sound of the dolphins.

"He urinates on us," he says softly, "and we poor, wretched creatures are helpless. They are all *El Campeón* and we are *los desgraciados*."

I do not bother to argue.

With only momentum to carry us, we continue northeast at a brisk pace. There is no conviction on the face of the Old Fish. He swims simply because he is a fish. A school of tuna sees us and scatters, but they needn't. The Old Fish has not eaten in hours. Why bother feeding a corpse?

Shortly before dawn, a weakfish seizes the blue runner the human has dangled from the rear of his skiff. Now there are three of us slicing through the water. Even a despondent marlin swims faster than any weakfish, and the surprised fish is tossed and pitched as we run. We make quite a sight, the three of us in the night, and I do not appreciate the laughter of the latin grunts as we rush past, nor their cackles of *"Vaya con la corriente, desperados!"*

The weakfish is screaming also, but we are going too fast for the Old Fish to hear her, until the buildup of Sargasso weed on the line slows him. When her cries become audible, we hear that she is asking us to slow down so that she can free herself from the line.

"Free yourself?" the Old Fish asks as he turns. "You know how to escape a hook?"

"Of course," she gasps. "I am a weakfish."

I realize that she is right. Weakfish got their name because of their flimsy flesh that tears so easily. The name was chosen with a sneer; it never occurred to me that their weakness could be a strength.

"Watch this, you thick-faced giant," she boasts.

But before she can rip the hook from her face, the fisherman cuts his end of her line and it sinks unceremoniously past us like a dead eel. With no tension on the line, the stunned weakfish is rendered as helpless as we.

She stares at us, the line drooping from her mouth into the depths far below.

"You could tell people you're still digesting the last of a giant squid," I offer.

"I wish I had the boy," comes the voice from the other side of the water.

"Now what do I do?" the weakfish moans.

"He has not cut my line," the Old Fish notices, and starts to pull and thrash at it, saying, "weakfish, show me how to tear this." But following another's current is like chasing a wave into the shore. A long swim to die on the desiccated sand, as the wave folds and returns to the sea, because it is a wave living as a wave should. The Old Fish is a marlin and only a marlin. His is not the current of a weakfish, and the strategy only wedges the hook deeper into his face.

"*Salao!*" shouts the Old Fish, but it is a matter of current, not luck.

At some point, hopeless situations become funny, and the Old Fish and weakfish notice each other and begin to laugh.

"Oh, weakfish, we are in big trouble."

"I am worse off than you, marlin. I would rather be dead than drag this tentacle through the water for the rest of my days."

"Days is all I have left. You may have years."

"Why us?"

"Why us?"

"*Salao.*"

They are still laughing and I cannot believe the comfort one can find in the company of another in misery.

"If only he had cut your line instead of mine," says the weakfish. "But it is not me he wants. It is you. He cut my line to keep it from interfering with yours."

"Why me? What did I do to deserve this?"

The weakfish has no answer for this and neither do I, but does it matter? The Old Fish seems to be drifting farther and farther from what matters. He has not spoken of Atlantis for a long while, and the Red Tide seems a distant memory. From above, there is a rocking in the skiff.

The weakfish is the first to notice this. "He is moving," she says. "I have an idea for you, if you are willing to try."

"Anything," agrees the Old Fish.

"You have not the strength to tear the line, but perhaps the human does."

"But why would he?" I ask.

"I do not know if he will. But perhaps if you get him angry, in trying to inflict more pain on you, he will widen your wound and allow the hook to fall out."

"What do you think, Fishmael?"

"I think it is foolish. You are not a weakfish. I think we should sound."

There is more rocking from the skiff above, the keel of the boat pushing the water laterally.

"You will miss your chance if you wait," the weakfish warns.

"It is worth trying," decides the Old Fish, and with that, he accelerates in the water. From above, we hear the tumbling and grunting sounds of the fisherman falling over in his boat.

I must admit to finding pleasure in the thought of him with his big, ugly feet in the air.

We listen for his reaction but there is only silence. I think perhaps we have killed him. This gladdens me, though I do not know how it improves our situation. I have never felt vengeful before, and I am surprised at how easily the taste of it sits in my mouth, tasting vaguely of metal. But my hopes quickly fade when I hear the fisherman's response to our tactic.

"Fish," he says with gentle malice, the words arriving one at a time and growing angrier with each syllable, *"I'll stay with you until I am dead."*

"Uh oh," sings the weakfish as she fades a bit lower in the water, "now you have gotten him really angry."

"Fishmael," asks the Old Fish, "do you recognize that voice?"

"I was just thinking that."

"It is familiar," he says, "though I cannot place it."

"God let him jump. I have enough line to handle him."

"Am I a fool, human?" the Old Fish frowns, looking up toward the surface.

The weakfish has been busily rolling herself along the length of the cut line. Only a bit of it dangles now; the rest of it she has wrapped about her torso. I am very impressed with her. She has recreated the tension on the line and will now surely tear herself free. My respect for her is short-lived, however.

"Not bad," she considers with satisfaction as she looks over the entwined line. "A little painful in the mouth but a rather serviceable shell. Well, Old Fish, I am off to study with the loggerheads. Do not worry, I am sure everything will turn out for the best. Swim with the current."

"Swim with the current," I answer, unsure of how this will turn out for the best and annoyed by the cliché.

The Old Fish says nothing. He is still staring upward. "He urinates on me and I can do nothing in response. *Alabao*, what a failure I am, as useless to myself as I was to Migdalia."

"We must think," I urge. "We must think of a solution or we will never get to Atlantis."

"Ah," he dismisses, "who needs Atlantis? A lot of trouble for nothing. If I can just tear the line, I can settle for living with a hook. It might even help me hunt. Sharp as a shark's tooth, it is."

"Old Fish, do not give up. Humans have no staying power. He will tire."

As the red morning sun rises over the sea, more profanity slithers through the water toward us.

"Fish, I love and respect you very much," the fisherman mocks, then turns his voice spitting and venomous. *"But I will kill you dead before this day ends."*

"I know that voice," says the Old Fish.

"I would like to see him try such a statement on land," I add.

"Is all the taunting really necessary? He has already won."

"No he hasn't, Old Fish. It is morning now, the perfect time for us to stage our fight. Everyone knows humans are solar powered. Their energy wanes along with the sun. Think of the rainy days, when few even bother to come out on the water and those who do are sluggish and weak. Now he has been without his precious sun fuel for an entire night. We must deny him food fuel also, as he does to us."

"Perhaps you are right. Did he not catch a tuna earlier?"

"Let's swim closer to smell if it is still on board."

Even from the other side of the water, the scent of the tuna—dry and dead in the air—is strong. The fisherman is talking again, but quietly now; words we would not have heard from our previous depth. It is to a bird he speaks, which gives us hope that perhaps he is going insane.

"Stay at my house if you like, bird. I am sorry I cannot hoist the sail and take you in with the small breeze that is rising. But I am with a friend."

"Some friend."

With that, the skiff begins to rock again.

"He might be going for the tuna, Old Fish," I shout. "Now, run!"

"Pray, Fishmael," says the Old Fish, his fighting spirit returning. "Pray that I can knock him into the water and settle this in a fair fight. *Te tiras el peo mas alto que el culo*, fisherman!" he cries. "I am too much for you, and now I will show you. To friendship!"

He surges directly forward, and above I see a wake of white water behind the skiff and think, now this meager human will see what a great fish can do. As before, we hear the lovely sound of the fisherman's defective skull bouncing off every corner of his skiff. Past the sea-ceiling, I see a small warbler take flight.

"Old Fish please, may I cheer now?"

"You may," he smiles.

"I hope your puny hands are so broken you cannot eat the tuna, fisherman!" I yell.

"Something hurt him then," comes the voice.

"Genius," says the Old Fish, his confidence return-ing. "I have not eaten in a day. Now we will both starve, fisherman."

"You're feeling it now, fish," answers the human. *"And so, God knows, am I. I wish the boy were here and that I had some salt."*

"He would eat the boy?" I ask, surprised.

"He will be disappointed if he does," says the Old Fish. "I have it on good authority that boys are better without salt."

Now the sea-ceiling gurgles and we look up to catch our first glimpse of the human. It is only his hand that appears in the water—an old, weathered hand, with rotting fingers, curved like mako teeth. For a brief moment, I assume he has realized who we are and is extending his hand in friendship, willing to call it a draw and cut us free. But I am wrong. As the hand washes through the water, a trail of blood lingers. I can-not tell if the blood comes from the hand itself, or if the hand has spilled the blood into the water.

"He contaminates the water with blood," the Old Fish nods.

"Why?"

"Probably to attract sharks. A ploy to intimidate us. Never mind your tricks, human; the sharks do not frighten us for they are our brothers. You will have to defeat me by yourself and I am beginning to doubt that you can do it. But it does not matter who wins. That is not a young hand you have there, and we will both be dead in due time. Whether I welcome you to the third

side or whether you welcome me, it makes little difference."

We watch the distance for sharks but none appear.
I realize that if the sharks do come, it will be to our
benefit, as they can bite through the line. I mention
this to the Old Fish and he brightens.

"Why wait? Go Fishmael. Go and bring help."

But I cannot. We have traveled a great distance
since yesterday morning, and to swim fast against the
Gulf Stream is not possible for so small a fish as I. And
even if I did manage to get there, what assurance do I
have that the Old Fish will not be dead and gone by the
time I return? I have no love of this world that would
keep me here without the Old Fish. Should he die, I
have decided to duck into his gill cavity and die with
him. I tell him this but my admirable loyalty only
angers him.

"You are the reason I am on this hook," he argues.
"You and your incessant taunting. And now you self-
ishly refuse to help me?"

"But don't you find my loyalty admirable?"

"I find you exasperating, Fishmael."

We had suspected earlier that the fisherman had
been going insane, and now we get our proof.

"What kind of hand is that?" we hear him say.
*"Cramp then if you want. Make yourself into a claw. It
will do you no good."*

"What does he mean, 'it will do you no good'?" I ask.

The Old Fish and I wait silently and listen to the
sound of chewing from the other side.

"How do you feel, hand? I'll eat some more for you."

"Old Fish, please tell me the wahoo is not eating his own hand."

There is a spitting sound and the sea-ceiling is shattered by the chunk of chewed skin that hits it.

"How does it go, hand? Or is too early to know?"

"Dios mio!" gasps the Old Fish. "He is worse than a tiger shark."

"We have no chance, we have no chance."

"That voice," the Old Fish repeats as the morning sun sheds its orange glow and rises yellow over the sea, "I know that voice."

Our speed increases slightly with the rising wind from the east. We are on course for Atlantis but still far away. The bright yellow sun fades slightly behind high clouds. There is a rainbow on the horizon but it dies as it submerges beneath the water surface, blending into white light. We get no rainbows under water; God made no promises to us.

"Be patient hand," says the fisherman. *"I do this for you."*

"I thought he ate that hand," I say.

A look of horror spreads over the face of the Old Fish. "No," he whispers. "It cannot be."

I am afraid to ask what he has just heard that I missed. We swim in silence for a moment, listening. The Old Fish's eyes are cast suspiciously upward. Finally, the fisherman speaks again.

"Now you can let the cord go, hand, and I will handle him with the right arm alone until you stop that nonsense."

"Fishmael, we are doomed."

The Old Fish has come nearly to a full stop in the water.

"What is it, Old Fish?"

"It is him."

"Who?"

"I know the voice now," he shudders. "It is *El Campeón*."

"Old Fish, you are imagining things."

"No, Fishmael. You too recognized the voice. Do you not remember how *El Campeón* talked to his hands all the while as he slaughtered Migdalia? He is the only fisherman I have ever heard do such a bizarre thing."

"No, Old Fish," I argue, though I already know he is right. "Your memory falters. He had another with him that day. It was that other human to whom he spoke."

"It is him," he repeats. "The most powerful fisherman in the world. We are doomed."

"But he is a fisherman," I lament. "Does he not realize that if we cannot stop the Red Tide, he too will die for lack of fish to eat?"

Now, please understand, I offered this more as an academic foundation for self-pity than as a hope for the Old Fish to seize upon. But he looks at me as though I've just saved our lives.

"Of course," he exults. "That's it! The only hope against any human is to explain to them their own selfish needs."

"I am sorry, Old Fish, but I'm not following."

"We must present ourselves," he concludes. "We must break the surface and shout so that he can hear us."

"Present ourselves?! To the kindly old gentleman up there quietly digesting his own hand?"

"I told you, Fishmael, he did not eat the hand. He was just speaking to it."

"Insanity is no better than autophagy."

"Self-preservation, Fishmael. It is the one thing common to all species." The Old Fish is beaming, and I am starting to believe that the hook has stolen his judgment. Could his mind be far behind?

"Not humans," I counter. "They see only the immediate. Do you not remember the reports of the continental rafting in the Pleistocene epoch, when delighted squeals of 'Wheeee!' were heard coming from above?"

"No," the Old Fish insists, "he is one of God's creatures, like us. There is a brotherhood in that. We will break the surface, show him our beauty and explain our obligation to stop the Red Tide, and he will release us." He begins to rise in the water, even as I use my suction cup to try to hold him down. "He is one of God's creatures and he is good."

"We have no chance, we have no chance."

"Light brisa. Better weather for me than for you, fish."

"He is evil," I shout. "Hear how he continues to taunt us even as we surrender to his goodness?"

"He is one of God's creatures . . ."

I swim atop the Old Fish's back and push down as hard as I can, but he is massive, seemingly heavier up here on the surface than he is below.

As we break the surface, I am clinging to the base of his dorsal fin and his royal blue head shimmers in the sun. I look for the fisherman, but am blinded by the reflection off the silver flanks of the Old Fish. Seeing his purple back and lavender stripes, his scepter spear and great wise eyes, I remember how splendid a creature the Old Fish is, and my heart aches that there are those on earth who would kill him. Here in the air he is noble again, no longer the confused fish who laughed with a mere weakfish over their common fates. I am seized for a moment with hope, but it is a deadly hope, chilly and vulgar in its stupidity. But just look at us, *El Campeón*. Surely you have never before seen a creature more deserving of life. Surely you can appreciate, fisherman, our dream of the sky. Can't you?

The eyes of the Old Fish are hazy and weak. They squint against the glare. We linger on the surface as the Old Fish raises his head and shouts our mission and our dream.

I do not know if *El Campeón* can hear us over the roar of the ocean, or if he would understand us if he could. Or if he would care, even if he understood. While on the surface, I catch a blinding glimpse of the sun, to which we also cannot speak. Can the creatures of the land speak to the sun? Can they even speak to the other creatures of the land? Does the sun hear the cry of the lonely moon? Or is all of creation isolated from the rest by layers of silence? And even if it is isolated, does silence prove nonexistence? Is there not more to reality than that which makes noise? Must the search for truth be confined to a lateral swim?

El Campeón's response to our plea? An elated howl. *"He is two feet longer than the skiff!"*

We sink back to a fathom, our hope fading. For a moment there is silence from above. Is he reconsidering? Might he decide that each heart should die only once at his strong hands? But the mad heart of the fisherman beats with frozen blood, and if ever a hope died a violent death, ours does now.

"I am not religious," he tells us. *"But I will say ten Our Fathers and ten Hail Marys that I should catch this fish, and I promise to make pilgrimage to the Virgin of Cobre if I catch him. That is a promise."*

With that, he begins rotely reciting what I can only assume are prayers. His tone is flat. There appears to be no thought behind the memorized words, no emotion, no sincerity. Just words spilling from his mouth like water running off the back of a great marlin in the sun.

Faster and faster he speaks, mumbling singsong words of prayer. *"Hail Mary full of Grace the Lord is with thee blessedarthouamongwomen andblessedisthe-fruitofthywombjesusholymarymotherofgodprayforussin-nersnowandatthehourofourdeathamenhailmaryfullofgrace-thelordiswiththeeblessedartthouamongwomen . . ."*

"Human prayer," the Old Fish sighs.

"Bob help us."

"Blessed Virgin, pray for the death of this fish."

"What a thing to pray for," I gasp, but when I look

back toward the Old Fish, he is praying also. Unlike the fisherman, though, his words are measured. He is speaking to his higher place that all fish seek and none more so than my lovely old friend who dreams of the sky.

He floats stiffly forward, his eyes closed and his weary fins resting against his silver sides. ". . . forgive me for failing my brothers of the sea and my dream of the sky. But be charitable toward me, hooked by the great *El Campeón*. I had no chance."

"thywombjesusholymarymotherofgodprayforussinners-nowandatthehour . . ."

"Shine a light on *El Campeón*, that he might see God and fish for what they are. Show him before he dies, so that I might die to one worthy of killing me. And if I am to be taken from my sweet sea, may I eat once more before I am? May I hunt once more? May I see a Spotted Dolphin?"

"Old Fish, please stop this."

He looks at me sadly. "I am so hungry."

He arches his head so that his glorious spear points toward the surface. "Do you think there may be shrimp in the Sargasso weed?"

I look up. There is no Sargasso weed above us.

"Your brain is playing tricks on you again, my friend." I begin to cry.

"There is a sailfish, Fishmael. Kill him and bring him to me."

"He's just kidding," I call to the angry sailfish who looks at me as if I were bait.

"How about mackerel for the halibut?"

What a tragedy it is to see a brain operate as an involuntary muscle, to dominate the spirit and heart, and plunge a fish into failure before he ever has the chance to succeed. The Old Fish would never allow a fin to disable him like this. Why does he let his brain? It is his brain; he is not its fish.

"I am so tired," he sighs.

"Then let us sleep awhile. Night is approaching and surely the fisherman will need sleep also. It will clear your head."

"Why me?"

"Sleep, Old Fish. In the morning, it will be your brain again."

"Why did you have to tease Jotaro?" he mumbles. "It is all your fault."

CHAPTER FOUR

How did I get here? So recently, the ocean was mine. The future was mine. We had defeated the viper and been crowned king of the sea. We had set out for Atlantis, to save the sea and finally achieve our dream of the sky. The current was with us and the waters were clear. The sky winked at us as we swam beneath it, as if to say, Soon my friends, soon we will be one.

And then comes *El Campeón*, returned to destroy what little he left living when he last interfered with our current. What is this hook of his? Does it really have the power we are giving it, or have we created it with our fears?

What is this hook?

Is it the equal of our dreams?

Is it the equal of the Old Fish?

Is it the equal of our current?

Or is it our new current?

A current, as I have said, is an elusive thing. I claim no authority of course; I am just a remora.

In fact, tonight I am barely even that. Tonight, I am a marlinsucker without a marlin to suck. Earlier, as the sun faded from the sky, the Old Fish again blamed me for his demise. For the first time ever, I spoke back to him, words I now regret, words which have torn us apart. Go away, he said, just go away. So simple. But how am I to go away, when he is all I have ever known?

So as the light has faded from the water, I have kept him in sight in the distance. Every now and then, he looks back to see me still following. My presence seems to irritate him, but there is a small part I think I see—maybe it is just a part of me—that is glad I am still here. Periodically, he stops to consult with any fish he happens to pass along his slow, aimless swim. He asks for advice on how to escape the hook but all they can do is answer from the perspective of their own currents. The clown wrasses laugh and tell him his wrasse is grass, the glassy sweepers say, don't worry, Prince Charming will arrive and save you, and the sharks just congratulate him on catching a human.

I keep my distance and swim beneath the skiff. As long as I am not allowed near the Old Fish, I might as well listen to the deranged ramblings of El Campeón. Maybe he will reveal something about his plan that I can use to our advantage.

He stays busy for a long while, tying oars to the rear

of his skiff then untying them, catching a dolphin fish and clubbing it to death as I listen to the dull thuds. More death. The best-kept secret in the universe. Soon, death will drop its pane of unbreakable glass between the Old Fish and me, and there it will remain, a shield between two devoted hearts, forever. I hear a splash in the water, another sardine-baited line.

"How do you feel, fish? I feel good and my left hand is better and I have food for a night and a day. Pull the boat, fish."

Have I been a fool, spending my life sucked onto a marlin by my head? Chasing the sky when I cannot even outswim a reasonably fit tuna? But it is my current. It has always been so. How could I do otherwise?

The life of a fish who denies the current that swims deep in his bones is nothing but a fraud, a lifelong flinch. And my current is no less worthy than the current of any other fish. I might not be a white shark, with its glamorous life, but I am no nurse shark either. The nurse spends her life within a patch of soggy sand more narrow even than the limits of her sight, sifting for mollusks and clams, never bothering to expand her horizons. And they call me crazy.

Am I? Am I crazier than the jawfish, with his mouthful of eggs, waiting for them to hatch? Have you ever seen a jawfish when some eggs hatch while others are not yet ready? You want to talk about confusion, try hosting that free-for-all in your mouth some day.

Squid mate in packs of a million or more, then deteriorate and die right there, layering the seabed three fathoms thick with dead, flaccid squid, just to have the blue sharks swoop in and devour them all. Same strategy every year. What possesses a squid to take part in this orgy of ten million tentacles, with death a certainty? Is the three seconds of sexual vertigo worth it? And how do they convince others to join them in their mass suicide? No wonder humans consider us stupid. But we are not stupid. We are loyal to our current.

And the blue sharks themselves, swimming in with their eyes closed and mouths open. Stuffing themselves with live squid, dead squid, squid eggs—probably ten pounds of sand and shells while they're at it. They eat until their stomachs can stretch no farther, to the point where squid are literally hanging out of their mouths because there is no room to swallow. Then what do they do? Do they stop? No, they force themselves to vomit so that they can continue feeding. But if they are full, why keep feeding? Isn't filling the whole point of feeding? Doesn't matter. Bulimia? No. Current.

Who fasts for months before they get to breed and, suffer into blindness, ulcerate their skin? And who sees their teeth fall out because they fast and die before they even breed? The eels. The eels. Current. The eels.

Current!

Eels travel in coed packs to distant breeding grounds, most dying along the way because they have been without food for so long. Coed packs. To breed. Wake up! She's right next to you! Why not get on with it? Why not indeed? I'll tell you why. Current.

Even the catfish, that hardheaded fool who cannot see past the tip of his moustache, has a current to which he is faithful. Is the catfish wrong when he tells us that there is no such thing as sky? Is he wrong not to jump himself? Or would his eyes explode if he jumped, so accustomed to darkness are they?

The current of the catfish is ignorance. The pain that light would cause to the eyes of the catfish is unimaginable. The catfish is correct to live as he does. He is living the current of ignorance in the most honest way possible. His misguided certainty is right. His assuredness that his bedrock perspective of the world is the only correct perspective is right. If he dwelled on the seabed but allowed for the possibility of sky, he would be betraying his place in the sea; he would be betraying his current. And in his most majestic fidelity to his current, in honor to all that is noble and true in the sea, the catfish not only remains ignorant, but he broadcasts his ignorance like gospel. He is audacious, dogmatic and absolutely idiotic—Bob bless him. The sea would be far better off if every fish followed his current so colorfully, so boldly. What benefit would the world gain from an ignorant shut-in? A reclusive buffoon would stand for nothing and deny the rest of us the opportunity to learn. So bless the loud fool. Bless the certain. We should cherish them.

In comparison to that, is it so bad to suck onto a great marlin and live off his hunts?

And now the Old Fish, my best friend, cannot find his own current and is ready to die. He is not the first fish to lose his current. I could help him find it, but he has no interest in my advice, even if my advice is to do exactly what he has always taught me.

When you lose your current, find your circles.

When your current disappears, there are only two places it can be. Either it has shifted, or it has met with an obstacle, a hook. Stay calm. Seclude yourself in a quiet place and chart your circles anew. If they have not changed, neither has your current; there is simply an obstacle to overcome while you stay on course. If, however, your circles have changed, and shrimp have overtaken balao as your core circle, give praise to the wonder of the great mother sea and stop looking for balao. Follow your new current with the same devotion you showed your last one. Or lack of devotion. I suppose compromise is a current itself, tepid waters through it may flow.

The circles are forever in flux. One must always listen carefully to them. Age is flux; health is flux. Why, today, nobility is my third circle and popularity only ninth. When popularity was first, nobility had no place at all.

One's current is a manifestation of his circles. Before Migdalia, love was not one of the Old Fish's circles at all. Companionship was fifth, but he always had me for that. When Migdalia entered his life, his current shifted because her love became his innermost circle. When she was taken, there could be no love, and so the Old Fish replaced love with hate. As dark as those years in the depths were, for one in search of hatred they were perfect. When the war ended, there was no point to being a warrior, and so we became scholars in search of the truths of the sky. When we find the truths we seek, perhaps we will live the sky without even thinking of it.

No, I have not been a fool. The fools are the schools of fish chasing currents that are not their own. Trying to be sharks, though the life of a predator would be the ruin of them. The sky can kill too. A whale who eats krill is always full, but one who dives deep in search of giant squid suffocates in its tentacles. We cannot all eat giant squid. But those of us meant to eat krill can fill our bellies more on that than we can on anything else. Krill is no worse than squid, just more krilly.

Life is not a turbid sea. It is a simple matter of current and circles. Every answer is somewhere in there. Somehow, I know that even the answer to the Red Tide lies in currents and circles, but I do not know where.

After all, I am just a remora.

The Old Fish is well ahead now. From behind me, I hear a voice. "I cannot believe he is still alive."

It is Jotaro.

CHAPTER FIVE

THE NIGHT IS heavy and I have not slept in days, but I recognize Jotaro's voice even before he emerges from the black water of night and approaches me.

"What do you want?" I sneer. "Haven't you caused enough trouble?"

"I mean you no harm," the boy answers. He lifts his left pectoral fin to show me something. It seems to glow white against the darkness. "See? I have recovered my egg and am now on my own way to Atlantis to learn the sky."

"What arrogance! You have no place in Atlantis. You have not earned the right to save the sea."

He looks past me to the Old Fish, who swims forward without taking notice of us. There is more sympathy than malice in Jotaro's wide, black eyes. "If not me, then who? The old-timer? He will never make it."

"He has fought more wars than you have dreamt of. He will make it." I know that this is a lie. The will of the Old Fish is broken, and he swims now more out of habit than choice. His pace has slowed, and his pectoral fins, normally pressed tight to his side when swimming at speed, now flare slightly away from his body. Still, his spear points forward, and until the day it points up, I will believe in him.

"Remora, I do not mean to offend. The Old Fish saved my egg. But look. Can you see the cracks in it? It will hatch very soon and I then will have a baby of my own. I do not wish to see it die in the Red Tide."

I am aghast. "You told the others about the Old Fish being hooked, didn't you?"

"No, of course not. I said that I could not keep pace with him. But I would have told them had that not worked."

"You would humiliate us?"

"Fishmael, there are twenty million fish at stake. You told me that."

"Who listens to me?"

He hovers in the water for a moment and stares at the Old Fish. Then he floats upward and glides against the fishing line to check its tension. "He is not even swimming at half speed," he concludes, more to himself than to me. "Even if I had brought sharks to cut the line, his days are through."

"That's right, sharks!" I exclaim. "Jotaro, go fetch some sharks."

"It would take too long. I must get to Atlantis."

"He saved your life! Your egg!"

"I cannot risk twenty million fish for the sake of one who will die anyway." He pauses and his gills flare wide. They look inviting but it is an illusion; they are not for me. "I should have ignored your pride and brought the sharks back with me sooner," he says.

I can see he is torn. "Jotaro, I beg you, please. He is all I have. Please."

But the young marlin will not waver. "I must go," he says, and tucks his pectoral fins tight against his body.

"You're going nowhere!" I shout, attacking him with all of my nine pounds.

"Get off me, you little wahoo."

I am no match for any marlin, but I fight him without fear of dying. Perhaps I am even in search of it. He swats at me with his spear, but I have seen him against the school of tuna, and I know he is not hitting me with full force. I want him to hit me harder; the pain feels good but not quite satisfying. Each swipe from his spear is liberating. The Old Fish has always fought for me, and I have never known the pure joy of placing my life in the current and screaming, Take it if you can; I am here! I swarm Jotaro, trying frantically to restrain him from leaving, demanding that he go fetch the sharks to cut the line. I curse my lack of hands as I try pathetically to suck him into submission.

"You just had to hunt for yourself, didn't you?" I yell, as dozing fish glance groggily at us.

"I saw you watching me. You let it happen."

"Take that back."

"Do not make me kill you, remora," he shouts. "I will kill you if I have to."

"You and what school?" I bluster, rolling with him and toppling about in our insignificant corner of the vast, salty sea. I can see nothing, and my head is full with the sound of rushing water. Suddenly, we hit something hard and smooth, and it jolts us from our tangle.

The fish we have toppled into freezes us both in wonder. It is somewhat larger than Jotaro, and so abounding is its beauty that it brims from its soul and pours phosphorescently into the water. Though tomorrow's sun is still far away, the waters around the amazing fish are lighted and clear. I watch as it circles to face us, its bold, turquoise water moving with it as it does.

Its eyes are small but they too are lit from within, like black pearls, and bubbling with joy such as I have never seen. Its beauty is different from that of the Old Fish. The Old Fish always found pleasure in his size and elegance, and that knowledge seemed to buoy his inner fish and strengthen his core. But while this new fish has no lavender stripes or Aegean blue head, it glows from its inside out. Its light radiates from its heart and shimmers past its smooth, dapple-gray skin.

"Wat is it boys?" she sings in a musical patois, then laughs a high-pitched staccato giggle. "Airen't there nut'ing better to occupy your time with dan fightin'?"

Jotaro is angry now, I think mainly because another fish has seen him fight a remora to a draw. "Shut your blowhole, porpoise," he snaps. "This is none of your business."

Again the smooth-skinned fish laughs her odd, chattering laugh, and the peals ricochet off the coral below. There is something magnetic and infectious about the laugh, and I am tempted to join her.

"Wo-yo-yo, I not a pourpoz, mon," she smiles. "I a dolphin."

Jotaro and I are dumbstruck. As Jotaro stares blankly, I spin full circle in search of the Old Fish, but he and the skiff have disappeared in the night.

"One of the Great Spotted Dolphins of Atlantis?" Jotaro asks.

I close my eyes in embarrassment at his recognition of the monumentally obvious. I wish I had an elbow to stick into him, but the dolphin's smile does not ebb.

"Yah, mon," she nods, "one an' de same, I and I." Before we can speak again, the dolphin flips herself over backward, rolling and swirling through the burnt orange coral below.

"Wait!" I shout. "Please don't leave."

Faster than a mako on a wounded sea lion, the dolphin is back in front of us.

"You were checking the road, weren't you?" Jotaro asks, his eyes wide and eager.

"How's dat?" the dolphin asks. I brace myself for the boy's explanation.

"The Great Spotted Dolphins are the Keepers of

the Road to Atlantis. Were you checking on the road just now?"

Kids.

The dolphin is amused by Jotaro. "It's just a road, child. Wat's to keep?"

"Why do you talk like that?"

"Like wat?"

"That singing thing you do when you speak."

"Jotaro," I interject, but the dolphin cuts me off.

"Tek it easy, mon," she sings to me, "de child deserve an answer. Wat you 'ear, child, is de music of de sea. Tis in you ahlso. Airen't it pretty?"

Jotaro smiles vacantly and I am grateful finally to have a chance to speak.

"Oh, Great Spotted Dolphin," I say, "I need your help. My friend, the Old Fish, he has been hooked. We were on our way to see you about some very important matters—given the blessing of all the fish in the sea to speak as one for them, but now we are hooked."

"Comin' to see me, mon? About wat?"

"The sea is in great danger, good dolphin, from the Red Tide. With your help, the Old Fish will save the sea."

The dolphin laughs and rolls, "Save de sea? Dat's a good one."

I feel a little foolish, but I am desperate.

"But the Red Tide is coming," I say.

"No problem, mon," she shrugs.

"It killed twenty million fish last time."

"Did indeed."

I am nonplussed. "Doesn't this concern you?"

"Not particularly, mon."

"Why not?"

She smiles and shakes her head. "Where dis fish I got to see? Tek me to 'im, come."

It is still dark when we find the Old Fish. At a distance, the dolphin slows and watches him. The Old Fish swims weakly, his head tottering slightly side to side, but he does not waver off his northeast line. The dolphin sighs, and I am right beside her when she says in a soft, somber voice, "Me see no 'ook, mon."

I look closely at her and can tell that she is not kidding.

"It's right there," I show her.

"Where?"

"There."

"Where?"

"There."

"Where?"

I realize there must be a more constructive way to use our time, and decide to change the subject. "Will you speak with him? He is no common fish, I assure you."

She shrugs. "I speakin' to you two, airen't I?"

CHAPTER SIX

TOGETHER, THE DOLPHIN and I approach the Old Fish, to find him sleeping. His slumber is deep, and he seems nearer to his old self in sleep than I have seen him for days. Still, his weariness shows in the flecks of brown that have appeared in his lavender stripes, and the obvious loss of blood and bulk from his flanks. It has been two days now of starvation, two days of struggle, towing the weight of the skiff. I move to wake him but the dolphin stops me.

"Let 'im sleep, mon," she smiles. "Can't you see 'im dreamin'?"

"There is no time to waste dreaming."

"Dreams 'is only chance, mon."

"Is it that bad?"

The dolphin smiles and turns to me. "Dreams your only chance too."

We swim astride the Old Fish in silence through the black water. Jotaro swims with us, a length behind. I try again to point out the hook now that we are up close to the Old Fish, but the dolphin still claims not to see it.

When the Old Fish finally awakens, he is greeted by the beautiful, smiling face of the dolphin. Still staring at her, he asks me, "Fishmael, do I still dream?"

"No Old Fish," I answer, and I hear my voice crack with emotion, "it is one of the Great Spotted Dolphins of Atlantis."

"Praise to the great mother sea," the Old Fish gasps. "My apology for sleeping through your arrival."

"No problem, mon," the dolphin says, her speckled silver flanks glowing brightly. Her tiny eyes sit directly behind her permanent smile, as though each holds the other in place. From here, I cannot tell if she is silver with gray spots, or gray with silver linings. But she is so much more than beautiful. "You was dreamin', big fish. Tell me 'bout your dream."

The Old Fish is still windstruck, but his eyes fade into the memory of his sleep, and through his agony a hint of happiness colors his face.

"I dreamt of the sky," he says wistfully. "I dreamt that I was a Spotted Dolphin amid a great school of Spotted Dolphins, jumping and playing beneath a bright sun. With every jump, I paused a bit longer in the blue air. With every jump, I went higher. A cool wind stroked my face and urged me even higher. Finally, I leapt far above the school and found myself floating through the sky, my fins spread like wings. And then it happened, what I have dreamt of all my life. I was flying! I flew so high that I sailed over the dry earth and black terns. I passed even the giant metal birds that sometimes crash into the water with their bellies full of the humans on which they feed. In time, my flight carried me to a small square cove built out of the dung of seabirds.

"There was a rectangular hole which I entered, bringing with me the chilly sea air. When I entered, I saw that it was the lair of *El Campeón*. He was sleeping. But it was not the *El Campeón* I knew, powerful and ruthless and always winning. It was a frail old man with scars across his back and hands, and the smell of defeat on his bones. His dream invaded my heart and sent a tremor down my spine, as though our sleeps were converging. He dreamt of me as I dreamt of him, and there in our dreams, for the first time, there was no line between us. I nibbled gently on his right arm to wake him, and he looked at me.

"I told him that he must rise and come learn the sky with me. That there was much to do and little time. But when he saw me, he spun and hid his face, crying into his chest that he was not ready to learn the sky. That there was a boy to raise. On a vast stretch of yellow beach, the strangest creatures I have ever seen— sea lions with legs—told him to join me. And I said, do not worry *El Campeón*, I will not make you fight. I will welcome you to the sky.

"But what I remember best of all was not what I saw or heard, but what I felt. Though she was nowhere in my eyes or ears, my senses were full of Migdalia. Her presence soothed me. It soothes me still, even now that I am awake."

The Old Fish does not exactly finish his tale; it simply washes away like a wave retreating from the beach, into the tranquil image in his mind.

"Sound nice, mon," the dolphin says. "Den you wake up."

The Old Fish casts his eyes away from us. "Dreams save only those forever in sleep. When I awoke, I realized that I am still confined to the water, still mutilated by this hook."

"I told you there's a hook," I tell the dolphin.

"Let I take a closer look," the dolphin says, then spins a dozen times around the head of the Old Fish. Her smile never wavers. "You ahl crazy. Me see no 'ook," she insists.

"It is right here, good dolphin," the Old Fish says, displaying his mangled jaw.

"Where?"

"Here."

"Where?"

"Old Fish," I put in, shaking my head, "trust me, this leads nowhere."

Suddenly, the dolphin disappears. I never see the wake of her turns, but from the corner of my sight, I see her below us, dipping and tumbling carefree and chipper. The Old Fish sluggishly shifts his body, trying to follow the impossible speed of the dolphin. Just when he angles his glance downward, the dolphin is back in front of us.

"How do you move like that?" the Old Fish stares.

"Dat?" the dolphin shrugs, "dat nut'ing, mon. How you move like you do, I wanna know?"

"Like what?"

"Dat dere stiff-sad-sad-swim you do, nuh."

In his youth, the Old Fish might have thwapped the fish who dared to ridicule his swimming. But the hook has stolen his fight along with his soul, and he drops his eyes. "As I say, I am indeed hooked."

"You just tell me you a flyin' dolphin, mon."

"That was just a dream."

"And dis just a 'ook."

"So you do see the hook," I shout.

"No, mon. Me see a teeny line couldn't 'old a tuna, but me see no 'ook. You can't tell me dis 'armless metal toy is de reason so grand a fish as you be swimmin' like he ahlready deaded."

"What else can I do?" the Old Fish asks. "It is a line held by the most dangerous fisherman in the world, *El Campeón*."

"Well kiss me neck-back, not *El Campeón*."

"You have heard of him?"

"Nah, but sounds bad, mon. Maybe you should get away from 'im."

The Old Fish and I looked to each other, not sure why the dolphin seems unable to grasp these relatively straightforward concepts. Hook, face, line.

"Is there any sound coming out of our mouths?" I ask Jotaro.

"That's not it," Jotaro answers from his distance.

The Old Fish's eyes brighten at the sight of him. "Jotaro!"

But Jotaro does not acknowledge him, only continues his thought. "Don't you see? The dolphin does not see hooks that are harmless, or hear words that are wrong."

"Boy not as stupid as you t'ink, remora," the dolphin laughs.

"You don't know him like I do," is my answer.

"If you blab about the tuna, Fishmael, so help me Bob—" but the dolphin cuts off Jotaro's threat.

"Dig fish," she says, "you strugglin' for freedom you ahlready got. You t'ink you hunted; you t'ink you flooded. Ahl you are—is free. Dat's ahl you ever been, freer dan you ever known. But you make a 'ook out of a jelly sting, a line out of a string, and a *El Campeón* out of nut'ing at ahl."

"You mean I can snap the line with a run?"

"You huge, mon. You fahst, you strong."

Without a word, the Old Fish makes a furious run, his eyes nearly closed, his fins pressed into the grooves at his side. But he is tired and weak, and even I am able to keep his pace.

"You finished," the dolphin says.

"*El Campeón* has defeated me again."

"No, mon. You defeated you. You and your traitorous brain. *El Campeón* not a match for you. Never was." The Old Fish and I look at her askance. She sees our doubt and glances up toward the bottom of the skiff. "You don't believe me? Den jump. Jump and see wat a puny animal you was up against ahl along."

The Old Fish obeys and I latch onto his belly to see for myself. We crash through the mottled sea-ceiling and fly into the warm night air, the wind a tickle on my face. I hear the buzzing of the flying fish speeding over the surface of the water, and I catch a fast glimpse of *El Campeón*. The sight of him is the most devastating light that has ever washed into my eyes.

El Campeón. Old. Weak. Small. And dying himself. Less of a match for us than a crippled flounder.

When we land back into the water, we are in shock. We feel foolish, a dupe to our own fears. What have we created?

"Whoo-hooh!" the dolphin cries. "Look at dem dere faces, Jotaro!"

There is a peculiar sting in my eyes, as though they have never felt saltwater before. Jotaro does not seem to enjoy whatever it is that makes the dolphin celebrate. He stares at us mutely.

"Jump again, big fish," the dolphin giggles. "Jump t'ree more time and see 'ow easy it is to defeat a tired old man." The Old Fish obeys, each time splashing back into the ocean, his expression darkening. Still, the dolphin does not relent. "Jump again!" she calls. "Jump seven more time and understand de danger of ideas."

El Campeón was no match for us. The hook was impotent. But so powerful was our idea of the hook, that it created a prophesy of failure all its own. The four of us swim in silence toward nothing, all waiting for someone else to speak. We were perfect. We were gifted, free lives. The current was with us. The waters were clear. The sky did wink at us as we swam beneath it. We knew our current, and had we only maintained faith in it despite the obstruction, we would by now be in Atlantis learning the sky that was our destiny.

It is the Old Fish himself who finally breaks the silence, as the soft morning sun shines gently over the sea. "I am doomed," he says.

"Tek it easy, mon. It's not so bad."

My heart fills with hope.

"You have a solution?" I ask the dolphin.

"Yah, mon."

"What?" asks the Old Fish.

"Die," she says soft and simple.

"Die?"

"Yah, mon. No problem, de sea will survive. Now swim your circles."

It is said to be a blessing on one's soul to swim ten concentric circles on the door of death, in honor to the ten concentric circles of life that guide our way through the seven seas. We will swim our outermost circle first, to represent the tenth most core value of our hearts. Then we will reduce each circle, swimming our ninth, eighth, and seventh in sequence. On the final circle— our dearest core and innermost treasure—we will turn and head west, so that we might enter our death mindful of that which truly filled our life with meaning. With resignation, the Old Fish begins to circle.

"*It is a very big circle,*" we hear from above. "*But he is circling.*"

"Poor old fish," Jotaro whispers.

CHAPTER SEVEN

D AT'S TEN," calls the dolphin as the Old Fish completes his first, and largest circle, that of ADVENTURE.

The sun has risen and the day is clear. I am suctioned to the Old Fish near his gills. My father once told me that the measure of a remora's life comes at the end: Will you forgo your own circles to accept those of your marlin? Are you willing to move not a fin, but simply dissolve into the circles of your life friend? I have given this great thought over the years, and I suspend my body as still as a summer sky as I adhere to the Old Fish and join his circles. I am near his gills, so that when he finally does die and is dragged aboard the old man's boat, I may go with him. Most remoras change hosts upon the death of their marlin. I think my father would be proud of me today.

"Why does the Old Fish swim these circles, dolphin?" I hear Jotaro ask as we pass.

"To know 'is true nature," answers the dolphin.

"Who cares? He is going to die anyway."

"Me still got 'igh 'opes for 'im, child."

"Hopes for what?"

We are beginning our ninth circle now—HUMOR—swimming away again from the dolphin. So I am not sure if I hear her correctly, but I am not willing to break my stillness to swim back and listen. Still, I could swear that the word she just spoke was "Atlantis."

Much time passes and we continue to circle.

"Dat's nine," calls the dolphin as we round the furthest arc of our second circle. The Old Fish is taking his time. The tenth circle took quite a while and the ninth was not much smaller. The dementia of earlier is gone now, and he swims proudly forward, steady and dignified. But I am his remora; I know that inside, he is terrified. Pressed against him, I hear the rumble of his empty belly and the thumping of his heart.

"Shall I bring you some shrimp from the Sargasso weed?" I ask him.

His answer is not directed at me, but to some other conversation which has been passing through his mind. "How is it that the only time I saw *El Campeón* for what he was, was in my dream?"

"Who can explain dreams, Old Fish? They are fanciful and unpredictable."

"Are they?" he wonders. "Or are they as real as that

which we call real? After all, *El Campeón* was real to us, was he not? And the boat full of powerful, fish-hating men, that too was real." He pauses and his head rises closer toward the surface, just barely. "Yet the only thing that was true came to me as I slept."

Sensing something strange in the Old Fish, I separate from him and swim to his face. His eyes are strange. It is as though a flash of lightning has shot through them, then disappeared as quickly as it came. The black eyes ignite twice more, then settle again into a blackness.

As the sun rises above the water, we begin our eighth circle, BEAUTY. Jotaro joins us and the Old Fish becomes angry when he sees him in our procession of death.

"Jotaro, go away. I do not want others dying with me out of a twisted sense of honor."

"Do not speak to me as though I were a fool, Old Fish," Jotaro says gently. "I have not come here to die. My life is devoted to my egg, I cannot die. I simply wish to know why you no longer care to live."

The Old Fish thinks a long time before speaking. "I would very much like to live, Jotaro—truly I would—but my regret is not the end of life. The end of life is life, just as the furthest end of my spear is as much marlin as my heart. *La vida es así.* My only regret is my failure to live my dream and attain Atlantis."

"Aha!" chatters the dolphin, appearing out of nowhere. "You on de threshold, mon."

"Of what?" I mutter. I am tiring of this dolphin. It is

not as though she has been of the help to us that we envisioned when we set out to find her.

"Why you gotta abandon you dream of de sky, Old Fish?"

The Old Fish, Jotaro and I share our first moment of community. We leave it to the Old Fish to speak for himself, however.

"Spotted Dolphin, surely you know that I am dying."

"So?"

"So how can I achieve the sky after I die?"

"You should try knowin' less, Old Fish. You been wrong so many time since even I meet you, 'ow can you t'ink you know anyt'ing anymore? First you say, me 'ooked, very bad. But 'ook 'as brought you to me and I are very wise, a Great Spotted Dolphin, doncha know? From Atlantis, the dream of your life and ahl. So maybe 'ook was good news. I show you 'ow easy for big fish like you to run and snap a little fishin' line. Of course, in starvin' for two days, you too weak to do it. Bad, dat. But I say, good news, you can still jump, and see what a puny animal you up against. So you jump and see a tired old mon. In fact, now dat I t'ink of it, soundin' don't take no energy. Why not sound and snap de line?"

"Because you already made me jump," the Old Fish answers. "The bladders of my belly are too full of air to sound."

The dolphin exults. "Now you gettin' de hang of it, mon!"

"So, in other words, you have just killed me."

"Bad news?"

"Yes!" the Old Fish cries in exasperation.

"Den bad news."

"What?"

"T'ink bad news, got bad news."

"But it is bad news. I am just trying to be realistic."

"Like you was wit' *El Campeón?*"

"Fine. Then tell me, what is the good news?"

"Good news?"

"Does it not end on good news?"

"You mean like, nut'ing 'appens by accident? Every-t'ing turn out for the best, and ahl?"

"Yes."

"No," the dolphin dismisses promptly. "Doze de words of a fool. Is dere not fluke in de sea, dem funny flat fish? De fluke a marvelous fish, mon. Unpredictable. Full of wonder, miracle and delight. Sometimes de fluke, 'e get 'imself in trouble—pain, 'ooks and Red Tides, doncha know. But 'e never stop lookin' for de sun. He make de bad news good and de good news better, and den 'e look back and say, 'Ah, good t'ing de waters got rough.' "

"The fluke is an admirable fish, it is true, always happy and eager for life. But how does that apply to death? Death is the end."

"It is?"

"It isn't?"

"It wasn't for me."

"But that's different. You died on Atlantis."

"I did?"

"You didn't?"

"No, mon, me die a fish, like you. But me 'ad an inner circle of purest love. Me live me life full and trust in me current, and so me soul stay in de sea; it did not go to humans to eat wit' mayonnaise. Dat's 'ow I become a dolphin. My life start when I die."

"That's impossible. Dolphins are reincarnated descendants of the lost continent."

"Oh, dat's impossible," the dolphin repeats the words of the Old Fish with a snicker. " 'Undred-million-year-old fish-humans, you believe, but 'ere is where you draw de line, eh? Tell me den, wat kind of lovin' God would sit back satisfy aftah he create a sea where everyone got to kill to live, and dat's de end of it? 'Ow possible is dat?"

The lightning crackles again in the Old Fish's eyes. "So you mean, any fish can evolve into a Spotted Dolphin?"

"But of course. If 'is inner circle is love and he leave 'is soul to de sea."

Tentatively, I ask, "Wouldn't that come under the definition of good news?"

"I suppose it would. Good, remora! You gettin' de hang of it. Of course . . ."

"Oh, no."

"What?"

"Well, you inner circle ain't love, tis life. Dat's why you clingin' to it like you are."

"But what good is love without life?"

"What good is life wit'out love?"

"Someone once said that to me."

"Migdalia?"

"Yes."

"Wat else she tell you?" the dolphin prods. Her words are an urgent whisper. For the first time, she is serious. Our plight no longer seems to amuse her. She watches the Old Fish closely, eagerly, with eyes full of compassion.

The Old Fish pauses in mid-circle and thinks. "To let go," he finally sighs.

"So let go." Her voice touches on the edge of pleading, but she quickly recovers.

"Of life?"

"Yah, mon," she smiles easily, nonchalant again. But her eyes glow with ice green radiance.

"But wait," I caution. "Good dolphin, your soul stayed in the sea because you sank. The old man intends to drag us out of the sea."

"I imagine 'e does."

"Unless . . ."

"What is it, Fishmael?" the Old Fish asks, as we begin our seventh circle, FAITH.

"Unless we gather the sharks to come and cut the line!"

"Go, Fishmael, go!" the Old Fish cries, as the dolphin backs away from us. She is trying not to betray anything, but seems disappointed that we have solved her puzzle.

I hesitate. "I cannot, Old Fish."

The Old Fish struggles for restraint. "Fishmael, I know you wish to die with me, but please, this is my only chance to learn the sky. I myself can be a Spotted Dolphin! Think of it!"

"It is not only that, Old Fish. I am but a remora, swimming against the current, no less. I'll never make it in time."

We both turn to Jotaro, who has tried to duck his head and hide.

"Jotaro," the Old Fish pleads, "do this for me."

The boy breathes deeply and I see his gills flare. "I cannot. I am so sorry Old Fish, but I cannot. With the egg under my fin, I cannot swim much faster than Fishmael."

"Then leave the egg here," I beg him. "I will watch it for you. Fetch the mako. She is our friend and the fastest shark in the sea."

Jotaro is as desperate as I. "I cannot trust you, Fishmael," he cries. "A hundred times you have spoken your desire to die with the Old Fish. If I am not back by the time he goes, you will not stay with my egg."

The Old Fish turns to me. "There is no cause for you to die, Fishmael," he says.

"Your death is cause enough for me."

"No Fishmael. *La vida es así.* It is time for you to find a new marlin, perhaps even a current all your own."

"You are my current."

"Jotaro would make a fine host for you."

"Your life was mine, your food was mine. So too will your death be mine."

"No Fishmael. Let my death serve you, not sacrifice you. To take the hook away from the boy was my decision, not yours. Just as my death is mine, not yours. You have no right to it."

"I would have no purpose without you."

"Yes, you would—to carry on our dream. Make it to Atlantis; learn the sky. Who says it must be a marlin who saves the sea? Why not a little remora? Let my name live on through your deeds. Fishmael, I beg you. Be selfish now, for me."

I am honestly not sure, right at this moment, whether the words that flow from my mouth amid a stream of bubbles are sincere, or a lie.

"I will stand by the egg until your return, Jotaro. You have my word."

The boy is torn. He looks younger than when we met him. "I want so badly to believe you, Fishmael. But this is my egg. How can I abandon it?"

I do not see the dolphin, but her words skim across the water like a cloud. They radiate through the sea, and I know that somewhere, a sleeping fish hears them and will dismiss them by morning as fancy. But when I turn to listen, the words are coming not from the dolphin, but from the Old Fish.

"Jotaro," he says, "we are nothing more or less than de gliding projection of our circles. They determine the life we live, whether we are aware of them or not. When I was just an infant, my core circle was love because I had not yet learned enough to lose my clarity. As I grew and competed, my core circle became life, and my behavior reflected that. Everyt'ing I did could be traced to my need to survive. I had no choice. Then

I met Migdalia, and learned that there is more to life than survival. But still, I fell short. While her heart was consumed by pure love, mine was consumed by her. The difference between the two is enormous. And so, when I could have washed my spirit over the sea and gloried in the beauty of our world, I instead lived in fear. Fear of losing her, which of course, I did anyway. Her death left me a shell, with but one circle: fear. With a heart full of fear, what choice was there but war? The Spotted Dolphin has shown me the way back to love. To the sky. Do not make the mistake I made, Jotaro. Love is a limitless commodity. There is no need to exclude others in order to love one with ahl you heart. If you truly love the egg, love the sea which gives it life. Devote yourself not to the egg, but to love, so that the egg may grow in a flourishing sea."

Desperately, Jotaro flashes toward the fishing line and beats it furiously with his growing bill. With each strike, the Old Fish winces but remains silent, all the while keeping his eyes on Jotaro. The boy's passion is for naught; the hook holds steady. I worry that Jotaro is wasting time and energy he could better use in swimming for the sharks, but as suddenly as he began, he stops. For a moment, he stares incredulously at the line as his breathing calms. With resignation, he returns to our side and gives me his egg.

He stares long and hard into my eyes. "Please Fishmael," is all he says before spinning and darting into the current like a miracle. He is out of sight in no time, leaving me to wonder whether I have lied to him.

CHAPTER EIGHT

WE BEGIN OUR sixth circle, TRUST, and are getting ever nearer to the old man, ever nearer to the surface. Are we closing in on the sky or the skiff? A female remora appears and tries to suck onto the Old Fish but I run her off. The Old Fish swims unsteadily, his gills opening and closing spasmodically. The wound has started to scar, and calloused tissue now surrounds the hook. The pain is probably duller now and I wonder which is worse, raw life or numb death. All I know is, I am soon to lose my mother, father, lover, brother, champion and best friend.

"Hold on, old friend," I implore. "Hold on. Jotaro is swift. Soon he will return with the sharks."

"Where is he? Do you see him yet?"

The sea has risen as the trade winds blow harder

from the north. It seems to be preparing for something. It seems to be trying to lift us out of the water, and here near the surface I can see nothing but whitecaps. I separate from the Old Fish and sound to twenty fathoms. I look eagerly into the murky distant blue, then return to the Old Fish.

"Nothing yet," I report.

The skiff bobs atop the water, and in a moment of calm water I can see the old man holding the fishing line. He wears a nest of some sort on his head, and from the look in his eyes, his victory over us will be short-lived. He is covered with saltwater, though the sea does not spray. His hands are as raw as the face of the Old Fish and they tremble and bleed as he fumbles desperately for more line. A man so intent on killing never notices when he has become his own prey. Just as well; I see no beauty in him, either within his pallid, colorless skin, or his lunatic eyes. I once thought I knew hate, but never has my heart been seized by such stormy blood. I try to drive the feeling off, heedful of the dolphin's warning: He without a core circle of love has no hope of Atlantis. I do not know yet if I will stay with the egg or enter the gills of the Old Fish when the time comes, should Jotaro not have arrived, and I do not wish to enter the distant mist with a heart full of hate.

I look down beneath my fin at the white sphere. A random network of thin, black cracks lattice across it. Soon it will hatch and another marlin will enter the sea. Perhaps it will grow to be a great one, one that my grandchildren will live off.

"Be calm and strong, old man," mumbles the fisherman, and from here, I can hear his voice clearly. There is pathos in it. I cannot tell if it is streaming out of him or into him. It makes me hate him all the more.

As though reading my thoughts, the Old Fish says, "Fishmael, remember: To eat, one must kill. Never let the fact that you have lived off my kill rob you of that truth. Do not hate the fisherman. He is like me, willing to absorb the stench of the kill himself rather than impose it on his remora."

"I cannot accept the nobility of one who steals my dearest friends. And steals the dream of Atlantis from you."

"We were so close," the Old Fish agrees.

As we begin our fifth circle, HONOR, the dolphin returns.

"Big Fish, you still so close. Drive de fear from your 'eart. Embrace your death."

"I must complete my circles," answers the Old Fish. "I must view for myself the core of love before I die."

We are higher in the water now, more close to the old man than I have ever been to a human. The human is pulling and praying and cursing and dying, but continuing to pull. Just barely, the Old Fish drops to his side, and the lascivious eyes of the old man widen. But the human does not understand the reaches of the warrior spirit, and is left gasping for breath as the Old Fish rights himself and swims away.

"I moved him. I moved him then."

"Fishmael, any sign of Jotaro?"

"I'm sorry Old Fish." There is a rattling in one of the cracks in the egg.

We curve slowly to our right and begin our fourth circle, FREEDOM. The circles are smaller now and pass more quickly. As we near the skiff, the Old Fish again falls to his side, only to right himself and again swim away.

"*Fish,*" comes the frail whisper through the air, "*Fish, you are going to have to die anyway. Do you have to kill me too?*"

Only a human could have the audacity to beg for mercy even as he kills.

"We were never going to save the sea, were we dolphin?" the Old Fish asks, almost amused now by our vanity.

"Course not, mon. 'Ow? Wit' laws and programs and policy initiatives? Can't be done, mon."

"So the catfish was right?" I ask.

"Catfish?"

"The Hardheaded Catfish of *Sagua la Grande*. He said the sea cannot be saved from above, only from below."

"Look mon, I don't know nut'ing 'bout no catfish, but de sea can't be saved from above or below neithah. De world work just like de fish. Nut'ing evah change except from de inside, out. Look closely at a ragged sea and you find fish. Look closely at de fish and you find circles. So to save de sea you gotta save each fish. Good fish can't make nut'ing but a good sea, an' bad fish can't make nut'ing but a bad sea. A free sea ain't de sea-ceiling, tis de seabed. Each fish gotta take it from dere 'imself."

"So we are all doomed," I mutter. "The Red Tide will come and wipe us all out."

"No Fishmael," says the Old Fish. "Listen to the dolphin. We are free. Everyone is. Red Tide does not hone like a shark. It simply comes, kills and passes. When it comes, simply leave. And tell the others to do likewise. They have no more hooks in their mouths than you."

"They won't do it," I predict. "The Gulf Stream is their home. They have built islands in the stream—schools, roots."

"Life's a pitch, mon. Tis a roll and a yaw. And when you gettin' flipped, flip. You can't fight de sea anyway."

Our third circle, CLARITY, passes much like the previous two. The Old Fish struggles to stay upright in the water, his back baking in the sun. He passes the skiff and the old man pulls him onto his side and celebrates, only to watch in despair as the Old Fish rights himself yet again and swims off. The old man is behaving oddly now. He spins his head in circles with his eyes closed and a foolish grin on his face. He wails through his grin and coughs his dry air, exhorting himself again and again not to go, though letting go is probably his only chance.

Once again I sound to look for Jotaro but he is nowhere in sight. The egg holds steady, occasionally rattling and buzzing beneath my fin. The dolphin is napping, floating unconsciously toward the surface every few minutes to draw air into her lungs. I wonder, if we dream of dolphins in our sleep, of what do the dolphins dream?

The eyes of the Old Fish are nearly gone and my heart is breaking with anxiety. Where is Jotaro? How could he fail us now? A mako can close on its prey in the time it takes the winged fins of a seahorse to beat once. I take the egg out and consider my responsibilities.

I feel little duty to Jotaro, he who caused this catastrophe in the first place. Certainly I do not owe him more than I owe to the Old Fish. But there is my duty to myself, to my own integrity. I gave my word. Then again, it is my own soul I risk. Do I not have the right to dishonor my life and legacy if I choose? Is that not part of freedom? And if I have that right, what better reason to do it than to die with the Old Fish? Of course, I gave my word on behalf of the Old Fish, for whom honor is the fifth circle. Is my treachery his? And could it cost him Atlantis?

I sound and swim away from the Old Fish. I am bursting to find Jotaro in the distance; I can see it so clearly in my mind. He is cutting cleanly through the water behind his hydrodynamic spear, with the mako on his fin and a hundred other sharks trailing behind. I hope Jotaro has had the good sense to cause himself to bleed, so that the slower sharks can follow the scent.

I strain my eyes and scan the infinite blue world around me. In the distance, I see nothing. There is nothing. I am afraid to venture any farther, lest the Old Fish die while I search and I miss my chance to join him.

Our penultimate circle is LIFE. Life, the most foolish, incurable circle of all. Dedication to it is a losing proposition, and every fish knows it from the first. But some commitments are too big to understand fully. You become sure simply because you decide to be sure. Because it is your brain; you are not its fish—it can be taught to absorb what helps and discard what does not.

"Fishmael, come closer to me," the Old Fish says. His voice is soft, as though coming from somewhere else. I am not even sure if I hear it or if after so many years, I am just able to sense his need.

This time, I do not suck onto him by my head. I swim up to his beautiful face and press myself to his mighty spear. I cannot believe it is possible for my heart to die a second time.

"Yes, old friend," I say.

"You have been a loyal friend," he begins. His voice is smooth and steady. "It was my honor to have a remora such as you. Forgive me for blaming you earlier."

"Take me with you," I plead. "Be it sky or watery grave, I want to stay with you."

"Live true to your word, Fishmael. Guard de egg."

"No."

"And when it hatches, tell it of I. Tell it of us." He pauses and his gills flare wide and slow. "Tell it de story of true friendship."

"Yes," I whisper. "Yes, I will tell it."

"And Fishmael?"

"Yes?" I weep.

"T'ank you."

"Thank you, Old Fish." We swim a final languorous, loving circle together around the skiff, reaching into the scales of the other and drawing each drop of love into our cores. In the distance, I see the dolphin waiting patiently. Gently, she nods to me, bidding me take my leave from my lifelong friend. She wishes to speak to the Old Fish herself, and so I steel myself to go. For a last moment, I hesitate.

"Old Fish," I say, "if you make it to the sky . . ."

"Yes?"

"Kiss Migdalia for me."

"Swim wit' de current, me brudda."

"Fly with the current, Old Fish."

CHAPTER NINE

M AKE UP YOU mind, big fish," the dolphin says bluntly. She shows no sympathy for the Old Fish, though he has reached his
innermost circle: LOVE. "Wat you gonna do?"

"Love be my core," answers the Old Fish.

But the dolphin dismisses him. "Ah," she frowns, "I
not interested in you words anymore, mon. Tellin' me
your core be love, but clingin' to life 'ard as ever."

"Then tell me, dolphin. How do I let go of life, truly
let go?"

"Just like you splash down after a jump, mon."

"But there's no choice in that. Gravity pulls me
down."

"Den let de sky pull you up."

"Will I reach the sky?"

The dolphin looks away, but the Old Fish persists.

"Dolphin, if you can promise me the sky, I can let go of my life."

"You got it backward, mon. Until you let go of life, you got no 'ope of de sky. Enough of your clingin', big fish. 'Asn't clingin' cost you enough? Was it not clingin' dat cost you Migdalia?"

On the verge of death, lying on his side as the old man raises a harpoon high above his head and readies to plunge it into the heart of the Old Fish, the Old Fish angers. Time seems to freeze: The old man hovering above with his implement of death, the dolphin surprisingly impatient, the Old Fish frightened and desperate. I feel a cold water gyre surge from the depths.

"What do you know of my Migdalia?" he demands.

The dolphin has stopped laughing.

"Big fish, I love you, brudda," she says. "But truth be 'ard. I know dat Migdalia's death cost you nut'ing but your constant fear of losin' 'er. Did she really beat you to dat 'ook, big fish? Or did you both know it was de only choice? I tell you a secret . . . ," her eyes widen; her voice shudders, "Migdalia knew."

The Old Fish is broken. It is as though we are reliving the day of her death. His color is as gray as mine, his eyes, two empty black windows to a ransacked soul. He flails pitifully in the surface water as the dolphin strikes her hardest blow yet.

"An' as long as you cravin' truth, big fish," she continues slowly, "den 'ere is some more. Dere is safety in dat dere 'ook and dat's why you sought it. You. Sought. It. It did not prevent you from anyt'ing; it spare you. It get you off de 'ook of 'aving to go to Atlantis. You been seekin' 'ooks ahl your life."

The Old Fish stares in horror at the dolphin. "What are you saying?"

"Why you t'ink for so many years, you not able to go to Atlantis and lairn de sky? Coincidence? Please. You dreams terrify you, and if not for de viper and de red tide, dis year too you find excuse not to go. So bless de 'ook and bless de fishermon. Dey bail you out again."

I realize that I am witnessing something I should not see. There is an opening here, I know, and I am being given a glimpse of some other world, some other sea. Time disconnects, and still the fisherman poses with the harpoon. Still the Old Fish lies on his side, skirting the worlds of life and death and sky and mud.

The Old Fish realizes the same thing I do. "Why are you telling me all this?" comes his wailing demand. "Why do this to me, good dolphin?"

The dolphin smiles gently, but her outer calm no longer hides her passion. "Because I need you in de sky. Me. I need you. An' because you smarter dan you know—you don't need Atlantis, mon. Ain't no 'ighway to de sky runnin' t'rough Atlantis. Aint' nut'ing in Atlantis but more water."

"Where is de 'ighway to de sky?"

I wonder if this is such a good time to be mocking the impaired speech of immortal beings, but then I realize that the Old Fish is not joking. The face of the dolphin is radiant. Her eyes turn upward and fix on the old man. Though the arm of the old man starts to move, the dolphin's aspect is pure joy. "Let go," she whispers, her eyes afire. "Find de truth in you dreams."

The Old Fish sees the harpoon descending. He is frantic. "But they are just dreams. They are not real."

"Trust me, mon, dey more real dan your fears. De sky is real; tis beautiful up dere, mon. Tis where God makes sense, and ahl 'is choices are kind. Up dere, even de Red Tide makes sense."

"Will me understan' ahl de mysteries that 'ave confused I down 'ere?"

"No mon," the dolphin chuckles, "you will be a dolphin, not a God. There are many more skies to be lairned yet."

"Me want to do it," the Old Fish declares, as the steel tip of the harpoon catches the sun and blinds me on its descent.

"Den do it," the dolphin exults. "Feel it. Trust your Migdalia. Let go! Climb back into you dream and believe in it like you believed in *El Campeón*."

The harpoon is plunging downward now, inches from the scales of the Old Fish, headed directly for his heart. The Old Fish is shaking, splashing, struggling, trying desperately to break free from his confines. To stretch his sight—not to see what his eyes cannot, but merely to accept that what is invisible may yet exist. To touch vapor and listen for silence. And to do it before his dream of the sky vanishes forever.

An electric eel passes underneath, glowing his glow.

"Be like de eel, mon," the dolphin implores. "Dat

dere eel t'ink he got a current ahl 'is own. An electric one, no less."

"But he does; he is an electric eel."

"An' you a flyin' marlin, mon!"

As the harpoon drives into the heart of the Old Fish, I am blinded by a flash of white light and red blood mixing and exploding, spewing a thousand feet into the depths. The ocean sways and rises, and I actually hear the steel harpoon squish through the heart of the Old Fish and twist into its core. Through the murk and boil of the water, I try to see what is happening, but can see nothing. I feel a surge of water beneath me, like a vertical Gulf Stream, rushing toward the surface. Something stings in my eyes. Suddenly, the Old Fish is airborne again, as in the days of our youth.

The water clears and becomes still. A pane of glass. I look through it as though it were sky. Beyond the water, I see the Old Fish hovering high above the fishing boat like a cloud. The old man stands with his back arched and his head facing upward, in awe of the Old Fish.

Then, as he has done a thousand times before, the Old Fish comes crashing back down toward the sea and splashes into it, dead and gone.

The sea is silent. Nothing moves. The dolphin is nowhere to be seen. The Old Fish is dead. And I am more alone than I have ever been.

CHAPTER TEN

WHEN JOTARO RETURNS with the sharks, I am hovering in the water in the same spot I have been since the Old Fish died. It is so quiet. I have never heard such silence. I cannot believe how lonely one less fish can make the world. Despite everything, however, I still have the egg tucked safely beneath my left pectoral fin.

I give it back to Jotaro. He smiles, then rests his eyes on me. "I cannot believe you really stayed," he says.

The fisherman has tied the Old Fish—or the hollowness that is left of him—to the side of the skiff. A white cord winds in through his mouth, out his gills, and many times around his body. He deserved to go with more dignity. The Old Fish is much longer than the boat, and I cannot stop staring at the mismatch. If only we had realized it. I wish I knew whether the Old Fish had found the sky. But the dolphin is gone now, and for prophets, the sea is once again left with misguided catfish.

"Fishmael," Jotaro suggests tentatively, "we must get to work."

He is right. I can mourn my own loneliness later. For now, we must cut the fishing line and ensure that the soul of the Old Fish remains in the sea, and is not chopped up for humans to eat with mayonnaise. Whatever mayonnaise is.

Jotaro has brought with him two mako sharks, our old friend and an acquaintance of hers. They are huge, magnificent sharks, with blue backs and silver bellies, and hundreds of teeth in their massive mouths. The scowl of a mako—its inert, black eyes and curved teeth—is perhaps the most terrifying sight in the sea. But this is only their appearance. They are like any predator, feeding and swimming. I have been told I have a bit of an underbite myself.

We ask if their teeth can bite through fishing line and they say, like it was Sargasso weed.

Our friend commends Jotaro on his speed and devotion to the Old Fish. She says that even as we speak, a thousand sharks are coursing through the water like a feeding frenzy, to save the soul of the Old Fish. She drifts upward toward the skiff to investigate and plan an attack. She has crossed paths with humans many times before, and knows that they can be ferocious fighters when their catch is threatened. Surely the old man will fight.

I watch the mako as she circles the skiff, and marvel at her gracefulness. Sharks are a miracle of evolution, in that they have resisted evolving for the past four hundred million years. It is through the sharks that the history of the sea is known, the Ice Age and continental rafting. Sharks are strong, fast and fearless. They swim like giant eels, their perfectly balanced muscles sending transverse waves down their streamlined bodies, their pectoral fins providing lift, their dorsals and anals, braking and turning power. Having no bones, they are light and effortless in the water. Their large, oily livers give them great buoyancy, along with the low-density jelly in their snouts. I have never known the fish that can outswim a shark, especially a mako.

We watch the mako circle and circle, until finally she returns to our side. "There is no line left to cut," she reports.

I realize to my horror that she is right. The old man has worked fast, lashing the Old Fish tightly to the side of the skiff, leaving no excess line for the sharks to cut.

"We must free him," I insist.

"It is not possible, Fishmael," she answers. "Even if our teeth were accurate enough to snip the cords without damaging the Old Fish, the fisherman will surely fight us all the while."

"But if he is dragged from the water, he will never ascend."

"You know, Fishmael," Jotaro points out, "that's not exactly what the dolphin said," but I ignore him.

"Eat him," I hear myself say, and none of us can believe that I just said it.

"What?" they ask in amazement. I am quite close to joining in with their question.

But whatever part of me speaks is sure enough of itself to say it again. "Eat the Old Fish," I repeat. "There is no other choice. It is his only hope of attaining the sky. Eat him."

The mako refuses. She says it would be an abomination for which her own soul would never be forgiven.

"If you love him, you must eat him. He must remain in the sea."

The mako does not move, and so I appeal to the other, who is less devoted to the Old Fish, and whose eyes look longingly at the sweet, thick marlin meat. It takes little to convince him, and in a moment he is sounded and ready to attack. I, Jotaro and the remaining mako watch in silence as the shark levels his body. His gills open to draw an extra beat of oxygen, and then they shut down as he accelerates toward the skiff.

Sharks are normally cautious predators, who will circle and circle forever, then bump and circle some more, before finally hitting their prey from behind. But this is not a hunt, it is a rescue, and the mako attacks the carcass with abandon. His lower jaw hits first, attaching itself to the Old Fish. I want to turn away but cannot. His upper jaw protrudes and tears down into the flesh of the Old Fish. He swings his head back and forth, tearing away massive chunks of meat. But his eyes do not roll back into his head, which comforts me. It means he is not in frenzy; he remains mindful of the nature of his task, and has not lost himself in the sweet taste.

As the mako simultaneously thrashes at the meat and fights the old man, the water grows cloudy. We can no longer see much from below, but the snapping of teeth reverberates for fathoms. I shudder and fight back tears as the water grows warm with blood. The fight on the surface becomes more violent and Jotaro moves as if to intercede on behalf of the dead marlin.

"No, Jotaro!" I shout and for the first time in his life, he listens to someone else.

By our side, the mako tilts her head to pick up the variety of scents.

"He has been hit," she says unhappily.

"It is necessary," I answer.

"No," the mako says, "not the Old Fish. The shark. The fisherman has hit the shark. It smells bad, like death."

We wait for what seems an eternity. The water is suddenly calm; no more thrashing or snapping. And then, sinking directly past us like a fallen angel, comes the carcass of the dead mako. The same harpoon that gored the heart of the Old Fish still juts from the mako's forehead. As he passes us, I see that he has been hit many times. Tiny blennies scurry to follow his descent and feed on the tiny fragments of brain that filter from his blue head.

"His belly was full," the other mako notes. "He ate much before he was killed."

"Fishmael, it is not worth it," Jotaro says.

"Perhaps you are right. It is enough death for one day."

"No," the mako decides. "Now the fisherman has killed too many."

"*I killed him in self-defense,*" the fisherman points out.

"He has a point," Jotaro allows.

"*And I killed him well,*" he continues.

"Brag, do you?" the mako seethes. "Well we will see. This is one fish you will not eat."

Just to torment us, the fisherman reaches into the water and pulls a plug of flesh from the Old Fish. We can hear him chewing it, flouting our grief. He makes all kinds of yummy sounds as he feasts on my best friend while we await more sharks.

In time, they arrive. Two requiem sharks, elegant and smart, charming fish if ever there were. They are happy to assist us, and they huddle their flat, triangular heads together to devise a plan.

"Okay," the first one proposes, "how about this? I'll go under the boat and start eating the underside of the marlin, while you attack on top, to keep the fisherman distracted."

The second requiem narrows his already narrow, yellow eyes. "Or," he counters, "I could go underneath while you distract the fisherman."

"What are you afraid of? You heard the remora. The fisherman lost his weapon to the mako."

"Then you have nothing to worry about."

This goes on for quite some time, until they resolve the issue and are ready to attack. Almost immediately, the one who had taken the upper angle slides past us in the water, blood streaming from his eye.

The other seems to be doing well under the skiff. We hear his chomping and tearing, as well as the hysterical cursing of the fisherman. For a man his age, I think, the fisherman should show more decorum. Then there is a sudden halt to the chewing sound, and soon, the second shark sinks past us.

"*Go on galano*," the old man screams. "*Slide down a mile deep. Go see your friend, or maybe it's your mother.*"

Mothers now?

"*I wish it were a dream and that I never hooked him. I'm sorry about it, fish. It makes everything wrong.*"

"He's apologizing," Jotaro says. "Can't we let it go now?"

"*I shouldn't have gone out so far, fish. Neither for you nor for me. I'm sorry, fish.*"

"He does sound sincere," the mako vacillates.

"Sincere?" I laugh. "He doesn't even know his real name. It's not 'Fish,' " I shout toward the surface, "it's 'Old Fish.' "

"Forgiveness is a virtue, Fishmael."

I think of the Hardheaded Catfish. I think of the old man's rote, selfish prayers for our death, the religion which was for him but another gaffe, a different bait. "No, my friends," I say. "Forgiveness is an excuse. Impenitence is the virtue. Impenitence lets no man off the hook. He probably apologized for Migdalia too, yet here he is again, back on the water, looking for more fish to kill. Clean slates are the ruin of man and fish alike. Only impenitence is noble. Only impenitence forces a choice between sin and self-respect."

A long time passes before the army of sharks arrive—mako, white, tiger, chain dogfish, marbled cat, flathead cat, false cat, requiem, hammerhead and bull. The skiff sails directly into the horde along the old man's return to land, and the sharks attack furiously. I stay below, yelling all the while, exhorting them, demanding that they carry the day and not stop until there is nothing left but the bone. Dislodged shark teeth sink past me like drops of rain.

Before the moon begins its nightly descent, all that is left of the Old Fish is his skeleton and his head.

I notice that the mako has not moved through the entire night. I wonder if she is afraid to die at the hands of the fisherman. But she answers my question before I ask it when she says, "Now, what I have been waiting for—the head."

"The head is barely digestible," I point out.

"I do not care. The fisherman will not keep the head."

I look around but all of the other sharks have already scattered.

"At least gather some of the others to cover you."

"I want to do this alone."

I position myself between the mako and the skiff.

"I cannot let you do it," I say. "It is too dangerous to go in alone. He still has the club."

"Swim with the current, Fishmael," she says, and darts around me toward the surface.

I give chase but it is no use. The mako goes for the head of the Old Fish without fear, and I hear the dull thud of the fisherman's club against her face. She is taking a terrible beating, but is determined to recapture the head. It refuses to tear, so thick and powerful is the bone. For a moment, she gets caught, her teeth embedded in the bone, leaving her vulnerable to the fisherman's assault. The old man wields a sharp piece of wood, and he lunges at her with it, driving it into her brain. I close my eyes as he pulls it out, and open them in time to see him lunge with it a second time, driving it again into her brain.

The mako rolls to her right. The Old Fish's head stays put.

The fisherman spits into my beloved ocean and cries, "*Eat that, galanos*," leaving me wishing that I, too, knew how to spit.

And then, the fisherman finally sails away with the skeleton into the dark night, and the sea sighs relief.

CHAPTER ELEVEN

I AWAKE TO a gray, dreary morning. The current is powerful and deep. The ocean rolls ominously beneath a blustery wind that whistles over the open sea. The sea does not welcome fishermen today. Despite the wind, the morning is the quietest morning of the quietest day in the storied history of the sea. But sometimes silent mornings are just evidence of a blaring night. The sounds of the battle still ringing in my head, I sense my current shift. This time, it is indeed my own current. There is nothing left for me today, but freedom dwells in that very void.

A school of timucu pass by and whisper to each other when they notice me. I realize that my new current is not virgin sea. I am still Fishmael, former remora to the grand Old Fish. Others will expect more of me now. My image will always be intertwined with that of the Old Fish. I will be expected to be worthy of his memory. I appreciate the responsibility; it offers the opportunity to become more than I am now.

The gore of last night has either sunk or been fed on by now, and the sea is once again clear. No longer is the water thick with blood, and for the first time in days, death does not weigh on my mind. But I am weary. I am relieved, incomplete, grateful and lost. Still, the sea is clear and I know my circles, and what more does a fish need?

Jotaro grants me little time with this pleasant thought, reminding me that death is still on the march.

"Fishmael," he says, appearing on my right flank, "wake up. We have much to do."

I am surprised to find him still here. I am more surprised to see, swimming awkwardly by his side, an infant marlin. The egg is gone. The hexagonal scales are visible along the sides of the baby. It will be many months before they embed in his skin. His two jaws are even; he has not yet even begun to grow a spear. His large, curious eyes watch me. Everything is new to him today. As far as he is concerned, the earth today took its very first revolution. There are no vipers, no *Campeónes,* no Old Fish.

He will hear of the Old Fish throughout his life, but it will never be more than a story to him, a gathering of words. Unfortunately, there are just so many words, and they have not yet invented ones capable of restoring a memory to flesh and warmth. The Old Fish was unique; there are no unique words.

"Fishmael," Jotaro repeats, "we must get to work."

"I am in no mood for chores, Jotaro. Be on your way now. Care for the baby, and swim with the current."

"You stayed true to your word, Fishmael. I am ashamed to admit that I was surprised by that. I was sure you would abandon my egg and die with the Old Fish."

"Teach him well, Jotaro. Turn him into a great marlin."

"I do not know what a great marlin is," he answers, and from the softness in his eyes, I can see that he means what he says. "Only you know what daily course leads a marlin to greatness."

"I must swim alone now."

"*Te lo juro por mi madre,* Fishmael, you must swim with us. You are still a remora."

The boy is right. He cannot be my teacher—my eyes have seen too much for that—but he is young, fast and strong. His spear is nearly full size. And he has learned to thwap tuna, not impale them. He will be a worthy host. I will be a worthy teacher.

The baby swims tentatively toward me. Soon enough, he will be many times my size, but for now, he is asking something of me.

I cannot reduce the Old Fish to words for the benefit of the baby marlin, so I simply press him against my side and let him feel the thumping of my heart.

"Do you feel that?" I ask. "That is the Old Fish."

He does not understand, but he likes the thumping and warmth, and he stays by my side. One day, he will understand. Not through words, but through the memories that continue to thump in my heart.

"Are you hungry, Jotaro?" I ask.

"Yes, but we have work to do before we may eat."

"Work?"

He looks into the blue distance. "Our currents have shifted, Fishmael, but the sea's current has stayed true. And now that the winds are high, the Red Tide will soon be upon the Gulf Stream. We must find the dolphin again and ask her how to defeat it."

I shake my tired, gray head. "No," I say. Jotaro looks at me with curiosity. "The Red Tide is not a thing to be defeated; it is a thing to be avoided. The fish of the Gulf Stream are free. All fish are free. They have no hooks in their mouths. All we must do is tell them to leave the Stream for a while."

"They will never do it," Jotaro protests.

"Of course not. Most will die."

I have no doubt that this prediction will come true. But it is not merely our destinies that are encircled. The entire world is a circle, as are the paths of all that inhabit it. And what is irony but a glance over your dorsal fin to see the most distant arc of your circle swimming close behind? The Old Fish sought to save the sea from the Red Tide. The old man killed the Old Fish before he could do this. The Red Tide will kill many fish for many months and the others will flee. The old fisherman and his town will starve for lack of fish.

None of the humans will see this, for the full circle is rarely revealed in this life. One day, one fish or man may find enough sky to see the earth from the vantage point of distance and clarity, and he will remark on the irony of it all. He will be a sage, but everyone will call him a dreamer and advise him to accept reality.

Last night, I dreamed of the Old Fish. In the dream, I was visited by a Great Spotted Dolphin, but beneath his translucent skin, hovering inside, I could see the face of the Old Fish. By his side was the dolphin who came to us to show the Old Fish the way to the sky. Beneath her skin was Migdalia.

"I am sorry I could not take you along also, Fish-mael," she says. "Your heart is not yet ready. But have faith in your current and, one day, it will be."

"What is it like?" I ask.

"What is what like?" the Old Fish asks.

"The sky. Is the water clearer up there?"

"It is the same," he shrugs. "It is the same perfect sea that you and I shared. It is only I that have changed."

"How have you changed, old friend?"

"Watch," he says.

With that, they ascend past the water with speed such as the ocean has never known. As they splash through the surface, the water sparkles and chimes, parting to let them pass. I wait for them to splash down again, but they do not return. The sea-ceiling stays parted, to let me watch them fly through the air like seagulls.

Together they splash down into a sandy beach far

away, and swim in the grainy earth. Sea lions lounge on rocks offshore, and the Old Fish and Migdalia join them until the Old Fish turns to Migdalia and says, "Now, my love," and they swim over the town and hover above a small square of seabird dung. Their spirits waft through the roof and into the air of *El Campeón's* sleep.

I watch the old man stir and moan in his sleep. He lies curled on a filthy square and holds on like a seahorse against a strong undertow. He tosses fitfully as the Old Fish and Migdalia breeze into his dream. His eyes flutter as the dolphins enter with his breath and fill his voiding shell. A wrinkled smile creases his withered face and a drop of saltwater forms beneath his closed eye and rolls down his face. As the dolphins join his dream, their light illuminates the aphotic canyon, and reveal again the peculiar sea lions with legs that yesterday the Old Fish described to the dolphin and me. The two dolphins gambol with these odd creatures as the old man watches. But while he is worn and defeated, his eyes stare lovingly at the two dolphins when they finally break from their play and turn back to him.

"It is time," they tell him. "Come join us."

The old man hesitates. "I do not think I am ready."

"Do not worry," answers the Old Fish. "I will not make you fight. You are ready."

"I needed to fish once more," the old man explains.

"And so you have."

"I went out too far."

"You're going much farther this time."

"What about the boy?"

"They too will find each other."

"Why me?" asks the old man.

Migdalia smiles. "Our fates were bound the day you helped me to the sky. Now I help you."

"If I were not worthy of sky?"

"Come," she says, extending her lithe fin. "The answers await you."

Slowly, the old man reaches for her. The Old Fish turns to me.

"Fishmael, dear friend, dreams are real. Know your circles that they may lead you to your current; know your current that it may lead you to your dreams. Your fears are real also. Live with the idea of the hook and it becomes real. Live with the idea of the dream, it too becomes real. If you must believe in only one, choose your dreams. For now, they are your only fleeting access to the sky."

"It seems impossible," I choke.

"Yes," he whispers. "But in truth, it is inevitable."

"I miss you," I begin to say, but before I can finish, the sea cascades together again and the sky is returned to a muddled, distant fog. But now, there are no secrets.

As swirls the sea, so swirls the earth, so swirls the fish, so swirls the man. The sun sets and the sun also rises. The moon dies and the moon is born. Man and fish are but cells in the face of the universe. How could we live by different rules? We set and we rise; we die and are born. We are the universe. We are the stars. To clean the sky, clean the stars. And swim with the current, my friends.

I never saw a man who looked
With such a wistful eye
Upon that little tent of blue
Which prisoners call the sky

OSCAR WILDE
THE BALLAD OF READING GAOL (1896)

CENTRAL